To
Jane R=
With Fond Regan.
Happy Reading!
Alice Flower
1998

THE MYSTERY OF
MRS. MANNING'S GARDEN

by Alice Flower

Published for Alice Flower by
MOUNTAIN HOUSE PUBLISHING
POLSON, MONTANA

Acknowledgments

I want to thank my dear friend, Barbara Fegan for her enthusiasm and continued encouragement for my writing.

Love to my granddaughter, Erica Paige Flower, who read every chapter as it was forthcoming and offered constructive critique and suggestion.

Many thanks to my sister-in-law, Jane Flower Deringer, an author and creative writing teacher, who lovingly guided me with her knowledge and good advice.

My gratitude to my good friend, Phyllis Ritter, for many hours of proofreading and editing.

Much appreciation to my family and many friends whose expertise in several fields was imparted freely and wisely to me whenever I asked for their help; Helen Miller, Lois Gene Cohen, Dr. Alex Scott, G.W. (Willie) Campbell, Ed A. Laird, Mrs. John D. Montgomery, Robert Flower, Jr., Douglas Deringer, Pola Firestone, Susan Hoskins, Sandra Detrixhe, and my wonderful husband of many years, Bob Flower, Sr..

Author's Note

This story is a character study of two interesting people; an elderly, well-to-do White woman who hires a young Black, teen-aged boy to help her with her gardening and yard work. It is a tender, humorous, touching account of their growing friendship, affection and respect, spanning generations, gender, and race.

The plot is an original creation of my own imagination.

The people depicted within this novel are composites of friends and family members I have known most of my life, including my mother and my grandmother.

The town of Valleyville is a melding of many small towns in which I have lived or where I have often visited.

Some of the incidents and events are taken from happenings which actually occurred when I was younger.

For my dear Friend
Mary Elizabeth Montgomery
who was my Inspiration

Prologue

Atmosphere in the cramped jail cell was damp and chilled. Condensation dripped monotonously from the single air conditioner duct centered in the high ceiling.

Hot sweat of terror ran in rivulets down Jeb's back. He stared stoically at his trembling, brown fingers. Slowly he turned those hands and gazed at the calloused, dark pink palms. Were they the kind of hands to rob and steal, pillage and vandalize, he wondered objectively? Could they beat and bludgeon an old woman to death? In his heart he knew the answer, recognized the truth.

The interrogation had been relentless, on and on into the hours before dawn. He was exhausted, emotionally and physically. He could no longer think straight and desperately needed to sleep; but he was too frightened. He had told the police everything he could remember about that night. Eventually, he had lapsed into a self-protective stupor.

The handcuffs rubbed his skin raw. His wrists were so badly chaffed and stinging he wanted to scream. When he saw a drop of his blood ooze from beneath the metal, he became rigid and still.

Initially they wouldn't tell him why he was under arrest. Then his folks hired a lawyer who explained the charges filed against him. He was in extremely serious trouble.

They kept him pretty much to himself but the scuttlebutt was that the whole town was riled up against him, and his heart clutched in fear.

"Lord," Jeb despaired, "How did I ever get into this terrible fix, and what in the world am I gonna do to get out of it?"

Chapter One

The young Black boy stood partially concealed in the shade of a lacy Locust tree. He stared intently at the old woman on the porch. She wore soiled cotton slacks, a faded blue work shirt with sleeves rolled up to the elbows. A worn, frayed straw hat was pulled down slightly across her face. She lay motionless on a porch recliner, eyes closed.

The boy couldn't tell if she was just resting or asleep. She remained so still he feared she might be dead. Her arms and hands were tanned by the sun, not enough to hide the many liver colored age spots; and her skin was wrinkled and flaccid. *She looks old enough to have passed on,* he thought. He took a hesitant step forward. *Lord,* he prayed, *please don't let her be dead!*

At that moment, a fly landed on her nose. Her hand came up in a half-hearted swipe to brush away the pesky thing. Relief flooded through the young man. Still he stood waiting, anxious and reluctant to approach.

Moments passed as a brief, teasing breeze rustled branches, casting dancing, speckled patterns on the brick walkway beside the rambling, white ranch-style house.

"Miz Manning," he said softly. There was no response. He ventured several steps closer. "Miz Manning," he said again. No movement, even yet. He was close enough now to spot the hearing aid in the ear that wasn't covered by her hat.

"No wonder" he mumbled under his breath. "Anyone that old has got to be deaf as a post."

Under the porch chair he noticed two big golden eyes gazing at him. They belonged to a huge yellow cat lying beneath the woman's recliner. He didn't have much use for cats, never been around many of the creatures. Most he'd seen were kind of wild and ornery anyway. This one's stare was so piercing it made him even more nervous.

He took another halting step forward and raised his voice. "Miz

Manning." The level of his own voice in the quiet backyard startled even himself.

The woman sat bolt upright. "What....what is it? Who are you?" Her voice was hoarse and cracked some, but she didn't look frightened.

"I'm Jeb, Ma'am. I work some down at the newspaper after school. Your son, Mister Carter sent me up here. Said you needed a bit of help with your garden."

"Oh, yes...yes...that's right. You're a little late. I expected you to come earlier. What did you say your name was?" She seemed a little rattled and her words were spoken rapidly, taking him back a pace. He figured she was a might embarrassed being caught napping.

Absently the woman reached for her small, wire-rimmed reading glasses on the porch table beside her.

"I'm Jeb Jenkins, Ma'am. My Momma used to work for you when she was going to school. You remember her? She was Laticia Brown then."

"Well, of course I do. Certainly I remember your mother. How old are you, son?"

"I'm sixteen, Miz Manning."

She put on the glasses and peered at him. Not because she felt she really needed them, of course, for she usually wore them only for reading. But she sometimes used them when she wanted to give someone or something a good once over. If the food on her plate was often blurred, well, that was of little consequence. She had very alert taste buds.

Mrs. Manning looked at him with an intense scrutiny, making him squirm a little. She saw that he was tall for his age, gangly because he had yet to grow fully into his body. His hands and feet seemed enormous in proportion to the rest of him. *This one is going to be a very big man*, she thought.

His face, however, was the most interesting. It was plain and smooth with dark brown skin. His mouth was large and broad, as if it would accommodate a huge smile. But the eyes were what impressed her. They were wide set, a deep rich chocolate color, diffident, but with a look of curiosity and intelligence.

"Sixteen, is it? Well, you look as if you have a pretty strong back for sixteen." She stood up slowly, stretching slightly. The boy was surprised to see how slight she was, thin and wiry, but not very tall.

The long haired cat emerged from under the chair and stretched lazily, then wound itself around the woman's legs with head butting against her trousers, purring. Jeb was surprised at the loudness of the noise the cat made, like a low-key blender motor.

"What does 'Jeb' stand for? Jebediah?" She asked him.

"Yessum, but the kids at school call me Jeb. I kind of like that better."

It was the third week of May in Kansas, but the heat could only be called oppressive. It mashed at the house and land with the weight of hard concrete, making it quite difficult to take a satisfying breath. Now, the breeze had ceased entirely. The air was heavily laden with the garden scents, almost overpowering in the stillness.

Flowers surrounding the back of the house were planted in great bunches of rioting colors; intense blues, sunny yellows, flashy pinks, cool lavenders, and show-off reds. The boy didn't know many of them by name, but he knew he liked the beauty spread out before him.

Mrs. Manning noticed the sheen of perspiration on his face and motioned for him to come up into the shade of the porch.

"Have you just come from school?" The boy nodded. "I'll wager it's plenty hot there, too," she commented. "Sit down for a minute, Jebediah," she pointed to a porch chair. "I'll get you a hat. You can't work in this heat with that sun bearing down on you. Not without something to cover your head, you can't."

The cat moved toward him as he approached the porch, which stopped him in his tracks. "Oh, that's Daisy," Mrs. Manning said, smiling. "She's the manager. Daisy thinks everything that goes on around here falls under her jurisdiction. She'll look over every inch of you and sniff you good before you'll get her approval." She opened the screen and stepped into the house.

Wouldn't you know it, Jeb mused, *a woman with a yard chock full of flowers would name her pet cat after one of them.* He didn't know what to think about that; but he sat gingerly on the edge of the chair to which she had directed him. He eyed the cat who returned his look without blinking.

His nose detected certain scents he thought he recognized. Somewhere out there among all those blooming things he could distinguish the sweet, distinctive smell of Honeysuckle.

He knew it well enough because many times when he and his brothers were younger, they had tasted the one sweet, sticky drop on the end of the stamen of those blossoms. Often when they came across Honeysuckle in bloom, they had stood for long moments savoring the small treasure from the heart of those flowers. Of course, most times they had some stiff competition from bees. He couldn't fault the bees, though. After all, that was their job and the reward was delicious.

Another odor he detected closer to him was that of Marigolds. He recognized that smell, too, because his Momma had some planted in the yard at home. Jeb never had been able to understand how those pretty things with their frilly, bright yellow, gold, and orange faces could have that strong, skunky smell. He thought nature had pulled a practical joke on them.

Jeb moved his knee over a bit, noticing a thorn caught on the leg of his jeans. He reached to dislodge it and saw the lovely deep pink flower at the end of the stem. A rose, he realized, and reached tentatively to touch the silken petals. His big hand cupped the flower carefully and his thumb gently stroked the beauty. "Soft," he marvelled. "So soft and smooth. Just like a baby's cheek."

Daisy, having made her appraisal, jumped soundlessly into his lap, startling him. His other hand found the back of Daisy's neck and he began to slowly stroke the fur behind her ears. This was evidently just what she had in mind because the low, buzzing purr began to emanate from her.

The woman, standing just inside the house at the screen door, regarded him as he had watched her earlier. She saw the fragile rose laid against his large palm and noted the tenderness with which he handled it. She realized how gently he patted Daisy and how the cat rubbed her face against his knees.

I was right, she thought, nodding her head in agreement with herself and Daisy, and her first impression of this child. *This is a live one. One I can teach. One who can learn. One with integrity.*

Mrs. Manning stepped onto the porch and handed Jeb the straw hat she had brought for him to wear as protection against the sun's harsh, glaring heat. Jeb accepted it reluctantly. As he looked dubiously at the ancient, mangy, and ragged thing, a smile barely cracked at the corners of his mouth. He perched it carefully on top of his close-cropped hair. Lord, he hoped none of his friends would ever catch him wearing this old thing!

"Now, let's get to work, Jebediah. Take this pair of garden gloves, too. You'll need them for handling the prickly things."

He struggled to get the gloves on. They fit too snugly, nearly cutting off the circulation in his hands. This fact didn't escape Mrs. Manning's notice.

"Never mind the gloves, Jebediah. We probably won't need them today, anyway." She made a mental note to get a bigger pair the first chance she got.

They walked down the porch steps and proceeded to the area where Mrs. Manning thought to begin Jeb's indoctrination into the garden. Daisy meandered slowly after them with her tail held high like a standard, exhibiting her best managerial strut.

Mrs. Manning hesitated, wondering if she should warn him so early on. Best to get it out of the way as soon as possible, she believed. She took a deep breath and said casually, "Jebediah, just so you're warned ahead of time. Please don't go anywhere near the cistern."

"Yessum," Jeb answered, puzzled. He had not a single notion what a cistern was.

Chapter Two

And so it began with the two of them kneeling beside a flower bed close to the porch. She was instructing him about each of the flowers and how to tell the difference between the flowers and the weeds.

"The weeds," she said haughtily, "are insinuating interlopers. They have no right and no place in my garden and must be eradicated."

After that he started carrying a small dictionary in his back pocket so he could look up all those fancy words she threw at him.

Early on he learned the very delicate and easily bruised flower petals were those of Petunias, which ranged in color from purest white and buttery yellow to a multitude of pink shades, crimson, and even deep, royal purple. Little yellow and orange plants with broad, fuzzy leaves that formed part of a bed, she called Cowslips. Other flowers edging the beds, blooming in a multitude of colors, were named Pansies, and looked like little faces peering up at him. They made him want to laugh, giving him a good feeling deep down inside. He told her so.

"You're absolutely right," she chuckled. "I think perhaps they're my favorites because they make me feel that way, too."

The taller flowers at the back of the beds were pale yellow and lavender, called Larkspur. "Poisonous, if ingested," Mrs. Manning stated firmly. Later, he'd get out his dictionary. All of these bloomers were pretty things. Beautiful, he thought, with mighty, peculiar names.

And thus it went. He came three times a week in the late afternoons and they seemed to work well together. At first he had thought she wanted a servant; but he came to realize that her garden, with all the variety of flowers and plants, was a great joy to her. She treated each of them more like pampered pets, and all she needed was a helper because of her age.

He wore his own favorite, faded and rumpled baseball cap after that first day. Better not take any chances of somebody surprising him in that awful monstrosity she had given him to wear.

Every time he came she taught him more about the rich soil and the care and feeding of the flowers. Lord knows there were enough of them. In front of the house, on the side of the house next to the driveway, the back yard was a vivid color picture, full of them. There was even a small vegetable garden on the other side of the house, away from the drive. He had discovered two Honeysuckle bushes there out back on the far side near the lot line.

"Knew I was right! I smelled you sweet things soon as I got here," Jeb spoke softly to the nostalgic aroma.

Mrs. Manning's home was gracefully situated into the landscape on top of a hill with a view of the whole town of Valleyville. A long, sloping drive curved up the steep incline and around in a circle to the front door. The hillside itself was mostly grassy lawn which flattened out some at the bottom with a large, stone sundial in the center, away from the shade of the big trees farther up on the slope, which lined either side of the driveway.

"Those wonderful trees," she explained to him, "are Elms and Oaks and Sycamores, ageless sentinels of the landscape." Secretly, Jeb got out his dictionary again.

Planted among the trees and around some large, protruding, limestone rocks were flowers she called perennials.

"Perennial means, Jebediah, that one doesn't have to plant them every year. They don't die out in the winter cold. They just keep coming back every spring by themselves. Hardy survivors, regenerating themselves."

There were Iris' in all colors, Jonquils, Hyacinths, Tulips, and tall, pink, native Phlox. Among them grew different types of Sedum, yellow and red, and many varieties of Lilies.

"Now, these flowers planted as bulbs which look similar to onions, " Mrs. Manning had explained, "are ones that double or multiply each year until they get so crowded they can't breathe to bloom anymore. Then, every couple of years they have to be dug up, separated, and replanted so they will bloom again."

The cat had taken a proprietary liking to Jeb and followed him wherever he worked in the yard. Daisy constantly butted him for attention and often as not he had to sweep her out of his work area in order to get anything done. Sometimes he stopped to scratch and pet her, hoping she'd eventually have enough of it and leave him be. Once in a while Daisy became such a pest, Mrs. Manning put her in the house just to get her out of the way.

Mrs. Manning would rest Jeb every so often. Oh, not that he couldn't outwork her by a long shot. That strong, young man most certainly could do that several times over. But, because there was so much to teach him and such a great deal for him to absorb at one time, she didn't want to overwhelm him and befuddle his mind while he was trying to take in all the information she was attempting to impart.

They were sitting, now, on some rock outcroppings in the shade of those ageless sentinels she was so proud of, taking a break and just chatting idly. Daisy crawled into Jeb's lap the moment he sat down. Without his even thinking about it, his hands began to work on her and the purring began again, automatically.

"Miz Manning, how in the world did you ever think to plant so many flowers everywhere all over this big yard?" Jeb asked her in wonder.

"Probably because I'm a little bit crazy," she replied straight-faced.

This answer startled Jeb and he had to look right at her and wait for her eyes to twinkle and her tiny smile to appear in order to realize she was teasing.

"Oh, Jebediah, I think I have loved flowers since the beginning of time. When I was a little girl, I used to pick the wild flowers which grew in the fields around our house in Oklahoma and take them to my mother to put in little vases for me. There were Buttercups and Goldenrod, Queen Anne's Lace, field Daisies, pink, white and yellow, Violets, and Sunflowers. I loved them all. Drove my Mother batty, I expect. We had bottles and milk jars and whatever else we could find to put my many bouquets in. Some of us had allergies and we sneezed a lot, too," she laughed.

"When we moved to Kansas, I was a few years older and I tried with little success to transplant some of the wild flowers into the beds around the house. It must have been a relief to my Mother when I finally got discouraged and gave that up. Besides, the Kansas country-side was full of wild flowers, too, many of them the same as in Oklahoma."

Jeb shook his head and wondered just exactly how many years she had been at this flower-growing business of hers.

"Here in Valleyville, out at Freedom Hall, where I used to live when I was growing up, we had a gardener and handyman to help out around the place because the grounds were so extensive. He was very good to me and so patient. I'll never forget him or his kindness to me. His name was Manny Rodriguez." Mrs. Manning paused a moment to reflect on the man who had furthered her interest in her beloved flowers.

"Manny used to give me seeds from time to time. He would tell me what they were going to be when they matured and flowered, how to plant them, when to plant them, how to take care of them, and how long it would take for them to bloom. He would give me a little place of my own to plant things, and I felt so proud...like a really big girl."

"At first I would just scratch at the ground, because I was too impatient to prepare it properly. Naturally, only a few would come to maturity, and they were pretty scrawny at that," she chuckled. "But Manny simply wouldn't let me give up. Then, I began to get results when I learned that one must do it the right way. But I was so strong-minded and stubborn, the right way came about pretty hard, mostly with Manny's determination and persistence, I'm sure."

Jeb could hardly believe she would confess these things about herself to him. He thought most older folks tried to convince you they had always been mighty perfect when they were younger. This unexpected attitude confused him a bit; but it made her seem more like a real person to him, not just a rich, old, pampered lady. He was beginning to think Miz Manning was a real corker.

Every time he came, Jeb was meaning to ask her about that cis-tern he was supposed to stay away from, whatever it was and wherev-er it was. But she kept him pretty busy most of the time, and it was usually so late when they finished up for the day, he was tired and always forgot to ask her.

Chapter Three

In the beginning of his work with the garden, Jeb found every-thing very confusing. There was so much you had to know. But Mrs. Manning was quite patient with him and very pleased with his obvious interest and eagerness to learn.

Gradually he began to recognize the different flowers, trees and shrubs and how to care for them individually. He soon found that he loved the feel of the earth in his hands, the aroma of the rich soil, and for that reason scorned wearing gloves. He loved the pungent, earthy smell. He reveled in the resulting color and fragrance of the flowers he had tended. Some, he discovered, didn't have any scent at all. He knew that because he had sniffed at every one. They were all beauti-ful in his eyes anyway. He began to feel a sense of pride and owner-ship about them, just as Mrs. Manning did.

Some days when the work was finished, and they were both all tuckered out, Mrs. Manning would ask him to sit on the porch for a while to rest and cool off. She would fix lemonade which tasted very good and refreshing, although sometimes he hankered for an ice cold Pepsi Cola. Once in a while, she set out homemade cookies or cake and they would just sit and chat companionably.

Mostly they talked about the garden and how pretty everything was, and about what had to be done the next time. She asked him about his family and his plans for the future. He told her there were six all together.

"There's Momma and Pop, of course. Then there's my older brother, Eli, and my brother, Jerry. He's four years younger than me, and my little sister Naomi, who's eight and right much of a pest, kinda like Daisy."

Mrs. manning had laughed at that, and stated that all little sisters were pests at one time or other. She said she knew from first-hand experience, because she had been one. Both a little sister and a pest. Jeb thought it was right peculiar she'd admit to it.

He told her he wasn't exactly sure what he wanted to do with his life after he graduated, but reckoned he had a few years to decide. She said she thought he was very bright and should use all his energies and intellect to make the right plans for his life ahead.

Many things about Mrs. Manning surprised Jeb. She might be old, he couldn't even begin to guess how old, but she had spunk and stamina. He thought maybe she knew everything there was to know about things that grew in the ground. Sometimes, though, when they were just talking idly, he would ask her questions about other things and she always seemed to have an answer, or at least an opinion.

"Now, that's only one opinion, Jebediah, which is my personal thought on the subject," she stated. "But you are free to think it through and form your own opinion."

She was one sharp old lady. That was a fact. And if her body was getting slightly frail, her mind was as quick-snap as a bear trap. Mrs. Manning told him that one time a long time ago she had taught school. Lord, that wasn't any surprise at all! He should have figured that out for himself. She sure was one heck of a lot smarter than most of his teachers. That was for certain.

The only thing that rattled him quite a bit was her insistence on calling him Jebediah. Yeah, that was what his folks had named him, all right. Mrs. Manning said, if his parents thought Jebediah was a fitting and proper name for their son, then he should wear it proudly. He had always thought it sounded so stuffy and he hoped nobody ever heard her call him that, or he'd be a laughing stock at school. It might even be worse than if he had been caught wearing that ugly, old, beat-up, straw hat.

Once again they were taking a short break, sitting on the rocks above the lawn. This particular time Daisy was curled up comfortably in Mrs. Manning's lap. Jeb thought he better get something straight once and for all. He was still stumped by what she had said to him that first day when he came to work.

"Miz Manning, what is a cistern? And where is it? I've looked just about everywhere and I can't seem to find it to stay away from because I don't know what I'm looking for."

He noticed her spine straighten slightly, and she became very quiet and still. She said nothing for so long, he thought she might not answer him. This thing about a cistern had kept on nagging at him and he felt now he might have stepped out of line asking about it.

Finally, Mrs. Manning began to speak very slowly. "It's a long, long story, Jebediah. I think maybe we'll save some of that for another day," she paused meaningfully.

"A cistern is a reservoir, usually for water, but depending on the size or purpose, it can be for other liquids. This part of the country used to be extremely arid before the construction of all the man-made lakes and dammed reservoirs."

What Jeb thought of as her "teacher's voice" took over.

"These newer factors have virtually changed the climate here. The summer rainfall used to be quite infrequent and sparse, occurring in severe thunderstorms with torrents of water coming down on the land too quickly for the ground to absorb the life-giving and badly needed moisture. This mid-west area is often referred to as "Tornado Alley", as you know. That kind of intense thunderstorm activity seems to breed tornadoes both large and small but which wreak devastation on the land wherever they touch down." She paused for a moment yet again, and both of them shivered a little thinking of the damage those horrific storms can and have been known to cause.

"I've endured several of those storms very close around us that I would like not to remember so vividly. But I'm digressing."

Jeb thought about his dictionary in his back pocket but was embarrassed to reach for it. He was impatient for her to get on with it. Daisy moved silently over onto Jeb's legs so as not to show preference.

"Water is the essence of the land. Man cannot live without it. When rain comes only intermittently, man must invent a means to save it. The cistern is one of those ways. Many farmers have built cisterns because, even with wells, the cistern is an extra facility to store water," Mrs. Manning explained.

"Rain barrels were used for that purpose also. A barrel was placed at the corner of a house to received the water which ran off the roof from the gutters. This was "soft" water and was used many times for washing, and could be boiled to purify it for drinking," she continued.

"Many smaller cisterns were built next to the farm house or even on the back porch. That is to say, the cistern is dug and the back porch is built over it so that the water is available in winter and bad weather, and one does not have to go to the well which is usually father away from the house. Naturally, in those long ago times, well water had to be hauled to the house and to any livestock in buckets. A formidable job! These cisterns for farm and family use were deep enough or adequately protected that the water would not freeze in winter even in extremely cold temperatures." Mrs. Manning took a deep breath.

"Here and there other larger and deeper cisterns were built years and years ago, before there were many houses, when the settlers were coming from the east to find land and build homes in this area and farther west. Some of them built these cisterns like oases along the more traveled trails so that the next homesteaders coming through could have water and stock up for the rest of their journey. These particular cisterns are usually lined with rock or clay tiles to prevent the sides from caving in and keep the water purer and less muddy. Amazingly, the water in most cisterns is fairly pure because most of them have sand bottoms. At greater depth, the silt and other impurities seem to settle on the bottom and stay there. It was always wiser to take water from the surface so as not to disturb the bottom," she said.

"The larger cisterns were marked on maps so travelers would be able to find and make use of them. It is thought some of them were constructed in the settler's time, probably by Scandinavians, many of whom were skilled in this type of work, especially tiling. No one knows exactly how long ago."

Jeb found the next part of the story fascinating.

"The Indian tribes which inhabited this region, the Kaw, the Crow, the Potawatomi, got water from the plentiful rivers and creeks, for the most part, even when they were running very low in the dry periods. But we are pretty sure the one built on our land is one of those used by the people of the more modern and resourceful tribes from time to time."

Jeb was awed by all this history lesson and amazed she knew so much about it. "Yessum, Miz Manning, all that is very interesting and I'm glad to know about it. But, just exactly where is the one on your property? So's I can avoid it, that is."

"It's there, just below us, Jebediah, beneath the sundial. My husband felt it was so dangerous, especially for the unwary, that he had it capped off and that granite sundial placed over it," she stated in a flat, far away voice.

Jeb stared at the lovely time-telling stone close to where he had weeded many a day. "But why does that make it so as we have to stay away from it now?" he asked reasonably.

"Because it's haunted, Jebediah. It's been haunted for over a hundred years by the spirit of a Crow Indian."

Jeb felt the gooseflesh rise up all over his body. His eyes were as big as saucers as he stared at the large, etched stone. He knew, sure as shooting, he didn't want anything to do with ghosts.

As if she could tell what they had been talking about and sensed their feelings, Daisy let out a hair-raising yowl.

Chapter Four

Jeb's family was always delighted when he regaled them with tales of Mrs. Manning and things he was learning about her garden with its great many varieties of flowers. They enjoyed some of his slightly embellished stories about what he considered Miz Manning's little eccentricities. Naomi especially wanted to meet Mrs. Manning's cat, Daisy, because Jeb talked so much about her.

This evening, seated around the dinner table, they were all wide-eyed as he related the story of the haunted cistern. Jeb's older brother, Eli, poo-pooed the notion as old folks superstition and laughed about it. Jerry, being younger, was more of a believer and was awed into silence.

At first, his sister Naomi's eyes grew huge, but them she pursed her mouth and narrowed her gaze. Indignantly, she demanded to know just who had the nerve to think of haunting Mrs. Manning's cistern, even though she really didn't rightly understand what a cistern was.

Jeb's mother was a little doubtful and said, "I wonder how come she never mentioned it to me when I was working for her?"

Pop said, "Well, if it's so, maybe she didn't think there was any need to tell you since you didn't do any work outside in the yard."

The whole family batted this fascinating topic of conversation around for quite a while with no one coming to any positive conclusion.

The Jenkins' were a close family and, whenever possible, dinner conversation and the sharing of experience was a norm at their house. They lived in a two story home with a basement which was on the far east side of town from Mrs. Manning. Their house was painted yellow with white shutters, and was in good condition because Jeb's father worked on it every chance he got. He was proud of what he had attained for his family.

Every two or three years in the summer, they all went out and

painted it. Pop and Eli painted up high on the ladder and Jeb and
Jerry did the work on the lower floor. Laticia always painted the trim
because she was neater and took more care and pains than the rest of
them. She didn't splatter as much paint, either. Even young Naomi
was also pressed into participating in this family venture. She was in
charge of washing brushes and putting empty paint cans into the
trash barrel.

Jeb always thought Momma and Pop were overly strict with all of
them, keeping a tight rein on their children, the boys especially. The
three of them felt their parents let Naomi get away with murder and
spoiled her rotten. But Jeb reasoned fairly that she was the only girl
and the youngest, so that counted for something. She did have to
help in the house a lot, keeping her room straight, setting the table
and helping with the dishes every so often. The boys did those
chores sometimes also; but they were mainly responsible for keeping
the yard mowed and the trash picked up.

Ben Jenkins had been the custodian at the Valleyville High School
for as long as Jeb could remember. Pop had told them, shaking his
head, that in those days they were all called "janitors". He had
scrubbed out pots and swabbed floors day after day, grateful to have
any job when so many people did not. Now, after all those years he
had seniority and was chief custodian, as they were called nowadays,
things like that being considered more politically correct. He was in
charge of ordering all supplies needed in the caretaking work, and the
hiring and firing of those who worked under him.

Now that Jeb was in high school, he hated it that Pop was there to
keep an eye on him. So did Eli. It didn't leave any room for acting up
or even getting a little bit out of line. The boys felt restricted, inhibit-
ed, and a little sorry for themselves.

Their father would brook no nonsense from his boys when it
came to behavior. He had a good sense of humor, tolerated some
mild pranks and harmless jokes, but no tough stuff or goofing off.

His philosophy was based mostly on some of the experiences of
his own youth. He had been in a few unsavory scrapes as a boy,
arrested a couple of times with a bunch of ornery guys up to no good.
But he had been released because he had only gone along with the

crowd and was not found guilty of any wrongdoing.

One day, back then, he had come up short, looking at himself and where his loose and irresponsible lifestyle was taking him. He thought definitely, he was going nowhere. That insightful knowledge was surely not what he wanted for his future. After that self-examination, he had straightened up his act. He deeply believed that there was enough trouble in the world today without his family contributing to it and thought they all ought to be concentrating on a good education and learning to be useful citizens, contributing to the society in which they lived.

Ben Jenkins had come to believe that he, himself, was a decent human being, and that God had blessed him with a wonderful wife, the mother of the children of whom he was so proud. For this boon he was ever grateful and tried to show it by his own demeanor.

The Jenkins' family went to the Second Baptist church on Jackson street. Everybody attended. No exceptions were allowed unless death was knocking at the door.

Jeb and Eli often tried to get out of going but mostly to no avail. They both thought the Reverend Wally's sermons were "dullsville". He repeated himself continually, even when he was screaming and shouting, trying to keep the attention of his congregation. He was intimidating, to say the least.

There was that one time when Eli drank a lot of hot water to make it seem like he was spiking a fever and the folks had let him stay home. He had sneaked out to play basketball with some of his friends; but drinking all that hot water and jumping around in the heat had really made him sick, so he ended up paying double.

Their parents had found out soon enough where Eli had been, what he had been doing, and it really hit the fan. The grapevine in a small town is sometimes faster than the Internet. Neighbors ratted on Eli's whereabouts that morning and he was as good as done for.

Of course, Pop had never laid a hand on any of them. That was something else he believed in. Said he was trying to follow the non-violent example of Dr. Martin Luther King, Jr. Almost every time, though, when Pop went into his lecture, the boys wished for a whippin' instead. They thought it couldn't have been much worse and would surely have been over with sooner.

Jeb tried a few of his own wiles every now and then; but he began to think he wasn't as canny as Eli because he seemed never to get far enough along to get away with anything.

But there was that once with Eli, when his older friend, Hack, who lived down the street from them, bought some beer and talked Jeb and Eli into drinking some of it. They had thought they were pretty cool and sophisticated; but when they finally went home and tried to go nonchalantly to bed, Momma had taken one look at them and hit the ceiling. Pop said he could have smelled them a block away. That was the worst bawling out and the hardest grounding they ever got. The boys had been put on restriction for a month. Eli said they had about as much freedom as a baby in a playpen. Neither one had been in a hurry to repeat that caper. Besides, they had both been pretty sick at the stomach, to boot.

Sometimes Jeb kind of thought his Momma favored him a little because she was always taking up for him when he got into minor scrapes. But she, too, had a pretty strict code for her children and kept a hawk-like eye on each of them.

Laticia Brown had been working as a housekeeper for Mrs. Manning at the time she married Ben Jenkins. She continued working for her until the babies came along. Then she decided to remain at home with her children.

At first she began to sew for other people as well as her family, and gained quite a reputation as a fine seamstress. Then she added to that income when she began to bake. Now she was famous around Valleyville for her cakes and pies, cinnamon rolls and coffee cakes. Her family always enjoyed it when she was baking because the house smelled so scrumptious. They knew they'd be likely to reap some of the benefits.

When Jeb first revealed the story of the haunted cistern to his family, they had all been incredulous. Ever since then each one, in turn, had badgered him to get the rest of the story out of Mrs. Manning. He reckoned he was every bit as curious as they were, maybe even more so; but he simply didn't know the best way to approach her.

Chapter Five

When Jeb first started to work for Mrs. Manning, before school let out, the hot spell was unusual even for a Kansas May. During the winter, he had been hired to work at the daily newspaper after school, loading and unloading trucks, dumping trash, running errands; things like that.

Mr. Carter Manning, who ran the newspaper ever since his father died, came to Jeb one day and asked if he would like to help his mother with some yard work. The thought of working outdoors appealed greatly to Jeb, so he had jumped at the chance.

Now, with school over for the summer, he worked every morning at the newspaper and three afternoons and Saturdays in Mrs. Manning's garden. It gave him great pride to be working at two jobs and earning his own money. He gave half of what he made to his mother for the family. He wasn't aware that she put most of it in a savings account for him. The other half gave him some spending money for burgers and stuff. He did save a little change now and then, in the ceramic baseball cap bank on his dresser.

Mrs. Manning told him that it was quite commendable of him to help with the care of his family. She said it made her proud to know a young man of integrity. He'd had to look up that word later; but when he found out what it meant, it pleased him greatly.

Now, at the end of June, it sure was hot enough again. But every once in a while it would rain and things would cool off a bit, enough to make the garden work tolerable.

First off, he thought working for an old white lady was going to be a drag; but they worked so well together that he soon found a grudging admiration for her. He was surprised to think that he actually liked her and had a great deal of respect for her. Of course, to be fair, she had treated him like a real person, not just some teenager, but with interest in himself as a human being and with consideration and respect as well.

Many times she sent him home with vegetables from her garden; tomatoes, squash, spinach. He knew it was a genuine thoughtfulness and not just charity, because she often shared the garden vegetables with her neighbors, too. She was just the kind of person who always did nice things for a body, even if he couldn't stand spinach. He didn't dare tell her, though.

Jeb knew the Manning family must be pretty well-to-do, maybe even rich, considering they owned the town's only newspaper. He had heard tell that Mr. Carter's grandfather had started up that paper a long, long time ago, and bought up or started from scratch several more newspapers in other small towns. Even one or two in other countries. Somewhere in South America he thought he'd heard someone say. Down at the newspaper in town, he'd seen a lot of framed awards on the wall. Many of them were for a column Mrs. Manning wrote regularly several years back. That fact didn't surprise him any. Maybe sometime, if it seemed right and proper, he'd ask her about those days when she was writing.

Most of the time Mrs. Manning worked along beside Jeb; but once in a while she would come out in the yard dressed fit to kill and wearing a lot of jewelry that looked like gold and diamonds, expensive stuff it seemed like. He thought she looked pretty spiffy, too, considering she was so long gone over the hill.

"You're on your own today, Jebediah," she'd say. "I'm off to luncheon and to play bridge with the girls."

"Yessum," he'd nod. But inside he'd chuckle, picturing what all those old ladies looked like that she called "the girls".

Sometimes he'd worry about her heading out in that finery and all that sparkly jewelry. He figured she ought not to be seen out in public like that because somebody not so nice might do her some harm just to get a hold of those dazzly rings and things. Jeb really did fret about her from time to time.

Lord, he was getting so stodgy from being around her, he was beginning to act like a fussy old hen himself.

Jeb watched, motionless and mesmerized, whenever Mrs. Manning took off on one of these excursions of hers. She had a very large, fancy car. Backing out of the garage was a mind-boggling event.

She would inch the automobile in reverse at the speed of a sloth, barely missing the huge Elm at the back of the house. Jeb found himself holding his breath as she put the car into drive, and once again only crept slowly forward to the brow of the hill.

It must have been at that point her courage emerged, because her acceleration was that of a skier taking off from the jump. The car lurched at the top of the drive and raced forward at an alarming rate of speed down the curving, paved surface, narrowly avoiding the drainage ditches on either side and braking as if she had hit a wall when she came to the stone pillars on either side of the drive at the street below. Then, she always turned sedately into the traffic.

Only when she was out of sight did Jeb let out his breath. "Lord be praised!" he said every time she exited safely. He discovered, no matter what temperature the weather, he was always sweating a little after one of these episodes.

One thing that still vexed Jeb mightily was Mrs. Manning's persistence in always calling him Jebediah. He'd tried nicely several times to tell her he preferred his shortened name of Jeb, which is what everybody else called him. But she was stone deaf on that subject and wouldn't budge. He figured that was a mighty peculiar stand to take, considering her own nickname. Whenever one of her "girls" had stopped by for a visit while he was working, they always called her, "Mandy Lil". Now, whoever heard of a name like that for a rich old lady school teacher, he'd like to know? And her calling him Jebediah. He just couldn't see the logic in it. Lord, what he'd give to know how on earth she'd got that dumb, silly name.

Jeb would probably have laughed out loud if he'd known she had given it to herself at the age of two.

Chapter Six

One afternoon in mid-July, they were sitting on the wooden bench outside the back door, in the cool shade of the huge old Elm. Daisy was busily occupied in the taller grass next to the garage stalking a field mouse.

It had been quite a pleasant day for yard work. Not the usual hot heat of mid-summer, but fairly nice with just enough breeze to keep the sweat from running in your eyes and down your back while working.

Mrs. Manning brought out sugar cookies she had made, iced tea for herself, and an ice cold can of Pepsi for Jeb. The surprised look on his face caused her to comment.

"Did you think I wouldn't notice all those Pepsi cans in the trash, Jebediah?" she asked, smiling knowingly at him. Well, he had to admit he'd been drinking Pepsi a few times on his way to work.

"I don't approve of all these carbonated cola beverages everyone drinks these days. I don't think they're all that good for a person, no matter how delicious they may taste. But you've learned so much rather quickly and done such a fine job recently, I thought I'd reward you with something I knew was more to your liking."

He tried hard not to show how much this pleased him but he couldn't keep his smile in check. "Yessum, thank you."

Dumb! Dumb! Dumb! he thought. *Couldn't think of something better than that when somebody flatters me a little. I'd best grow up and learn to act more like a man.*

He felt right much like a fool. But Mrs. Manning didn't seem to notice. She gave him her straight-on-everyday-nice smile and said, "You're welcome, Jebediah; and thank YOU!"

Well, he still didn't know how to answer that either, so he just sat back to sip his cola and cool off and think about what all they had been doing that afternoon.

Mrs. Manning told him there had been so much to do and get

acclimated to when he first came that they were very tardy digging up all the bulbs they needed to replant sometime in the fall before a hard frost. So that work had taken up the entire afternoon. She brought a whole bunch of brown paper bags and a big black marking pen; and they went down the hill to the rocks and trees where all the spring blooming bulbs were "sleeping", she said.

Jeb was wary of how close they were to the dreaded cistern; but Mrs. Manning seemed unperturbed and disinclined to mention it. He figured, since she was in one of her teaching phases, and they were concentrating so hard on the digging and sorting, it was best not to bring up the subject at that moment. Maybe because it was broad daylight, she wasn't too much bothered about getting haunted. Besides, she was so busy giving him instructions she might have forgot about it herself.

He dug, very carefully, like she told him to do; and she named each of the types of bulbs and put them into the sacks and labeled them.

They had to shove Daisy away several times because when the loosened bulbs were freed of soil, she liked to bat them around like marbles. The cat also seemed to have forgotten their proximity to the cistern in the fun of the new game she had discovered. Mrs. Manning stated there would probably be a few odd plants mixed together next spring due to Daisy's help.

To him they all looked like onions that hadn't come to full grown for frying yet; but she shook the dirt off each one and handled it like a prize.

They put the marked bags in a wheelbarrow and he had wheeled it up to the garage. There was a special shelf built, suspended from the rafters in the garage.

"This shelf helps keep the field mice from getting at the bulbs to eat them, " she informed him.

Well, he couldn't blame the mice for thinking like that. They did look pretty much like onions; and he liked onions, even if they did make you cry and your breath mighty powerful. There was also a special exhaust fan in the side wall of the garage. Mrs. Manning said this served to keep the air circulating on very hot days, so the bulbs wouldn't dry rot.

Whew, he thought. *There surely was plenty to learn and remember about the care and feeding of growing things!*

As they sat now in a comfortable silence, munching cookies and sipping their drinks, Jeb wondered if he could get up the nerve to ask her about her nickname.

"Miz Manning," he said finally, his voice cracking in his nervousness. "You mind if I ask you a right personal question?"

She gave him a stern look, but said lightly, "Well, you have permission to ask it, Jebediah, and after I hear the question, I'll let you know whether or not I'll answer it. Fair enough?"

He nodded, swallowed hard and drummed up his courage. *No use quitting now when I'm so close to maybe knowing.*

"Well, you keep on calling me Jebediah instead of Jeb. How come when all your lady friends come to visit I hear them call you a kind of funny nickname?"

Mrs. Manning looked straight at him, her eyes real wide and twinkling. Then she threw back her head and laughed, a very big, up-from-way-down laugh. Jeb didn't know what to make of that reaction, so he simply sat real still and waited.

"Oh, mercy me, Jebediah, forgive me. Your question took me so by surprise." Then she took a deep breath and leaned back against the house, and seemed to sort of go inside herself a ways.

"I gave that name to myself when I was very little," she said softly, turning to look at him. "Would you believe that, Jebediah?" He didn't know if he was supposed to nod "yes" or "no", so he just smiled.

"I was born, Amanda Lillian Fairchild, in a small town in northern Oklahoma about a decade after the turn of this century. Just a few years after the territory joined the union as a state."

Lord, he hoped his face didn't show it, but he thought she ought to be old as Methuselah!

"I think I must have been the despair of my very genteel mother who tried valiantly to mold me into a proper young lady...because I was born a true rebel." She sighed and smiled a funny little smile, as if she enjoyed the remembering.

Jeb didn't mind that; and besides, he was pretty much fascinated by the story. It was sort of like listening to a live history book.

Mrs. Manning went on with the reminiscences of her young life as if she were talking about somebody else she once knew long ago. She admitted, with a certain shyness, that she was the pride and joy and the apple of her father's eye, in spite of all her youthful antics.

She recalled that sometimes when she was supposed to be taking a nap, they might find her in the blackberry patch with a purple face and a purple stained dress as well. Jeb chuckled at that. And when she should have been in the sun room learning to embroider a fine linen handkerchief, as girls in that day were wont to do, she might be found hanging upside down on a tree limb in the orchard. Or late in the afternoons when her sisters were learning the finer points of serving tea, they might often catch her riding bareback on the family's old work horse, "Whiz Bang", as fast as the tired old nag would go around the barn out back of the house.

Jeb really laughed trying to picture that. But he had a hard time getting a mental handle on Mrs. Manning ever being young enough to ride a horse or hang upside down in a tree.

"At two years old, they told me," she related, "I was prattling on a mile a minute. I guess the urge to talk was inbred in me from the start. From what my parents told me, I was obviously impatient with the time it took to learn all the words I needed in order to make myself understood...to communicate. That has always been important to me. Half the time, my family said, they couldn't tell what I was saying; but that didn't stop me. A regular babbling brook, I guess I was."

"When I was about two, I nicknamed my older sister, Mar Mar. Her name was Margaret Marian; but that seemed too hard for me to say. And my own name, Amanda Lillian...well, that was such a mouthful and took way too much precious time to spout out, sooo...I called myself Mandy Lil." She paused to laugh, a tinkling sound which matched her "story voice" that seemed to grow younger and more animated the more she talked.

Jeb was mesmerized just watching her telling of her childhood.

When her little sister, Sarah Leona, was born several years later, Mrs. Manning revealed, she promptly dubbed her, Sa-lee. Her parents tried in vain to correct all these "Mandyisms", but she was implacable.

Dr. and Mrs. Fairchild might as well have saved themselves the trouble of naming their daughters because Mandy Lil's nicknames stuck. The Fairchild girls were called "Mar Mar", "Mandy Lil", and "Sally" by everyone who knew them, for the rest of their lives.

Jeb and Mrs. Manning were quiet for a moment, reflecting on the storytelling together.

Then she said, "Does all that rambling about the past answer your question, Jebediah? You probably formed the opinion that I was quite a caution when I was younger, and you'd be right about that." Jeb grinned and shook his head. Then he looked at his watch and quickly stood up.

"Goodness gracious, Jebediah, look at the time. True to form, I've just about talked your ears off. It's so late your mother will be worried sick about you. Hop in the car. I'll put Daisy in the house, get my keys, and take you home."

Judging by what he'd seen in the past, Jeb was not at all keen on Mrs. Manning's driving; and he was loath to get into the car with the prospect of her at the wheel. He debated how he could tell her nicely that he didn't need a ride; but he couldn't think of a logical explanation, so he gave up. He reckoned as how it might be some better than a fat scolding at getting home so late...if they made it at all. Very reluctantly, he took his seat in the vehicle beside Mrs. Manning.

Chapter Seven

Mrs. Manning had a compost heap out back of the house, quite a ways behind the vegetable garden almost to the edge of the property. And Jeb thought it was a good thing, too, because that heap stunk to high heaven. She told him the compost was a magic, sustaining elixir which stimulated and nourished all her growing things to their uttermost exquisite fulfillment. Jeb understood the gist of that but thought the powerful smell could just about stimulate a reaction from anything or anybody.

Mrs. Manning didn't seem to mind being around the heap, though, and talked about it in glowing terms. She explained just what they had to do to keep it "working".

Yeah, right, Jeb thought. *I know who "they" is; and I know who she has this job cut out for.*

She explained that when the fallen leaves were raked up in the fall, a good many of them could go on the compost heap. As usual, she would save her garbage of potato peels, carrot scrapings, eggshells, coffee grounds and the like, and add them to the pile every day or so. Quick lime would be added now and then, and they would keep turning over the whole concoction so it would mix well and decompose more rapidly. Jeb had to take her word for it because his discomposure came from being around that foul smelling, rotting mess. Even Daisy gave it a wide berth.

Jeb did what he was told, however unpleasant the task. He figured it was all part of the job and there were so many other things about gardening he liked right much.

He had just finished this putrid chore one afternoon and was walking toward the flower beds by the porch when he happened to glance down the hill at the cistern. He stopped dead in his tracks, rooted to the ground in fright. There on the sundial stood a huge man with his arms reaching skyward, obviously in some sort of trance, chanting in a nasal monotone. Jeb told his legs to take him the heck away from this spot as fast as they could, but they simply wouldn't obey him. His eyes were about to bug out of his head and the hair on the back of his neck was standing up as stiff as a board. He couldn't have moved if there had been gunpowder blasted under him.

At that moment, Mrs. Manning walked out on the porch and said calmly, "Well, it looks as if we are about to have the honor of a visit from George Raven's Wing."

The man gradually lowered his arms and began walking in long strides up the hill toward them. Jeb wanted to yell, "Run, Miz Manning, run!" But his mouth and his voice failed him at the same time.

Mrs. Manning stepped from the porch and stuck out her hand to shake that of the visitor. "Hello, George. It's been a long time."

The man clasped her hand, which vanished in both his large ones. "Amanda, child. It's good to see you." A gruff resonant voice resounded from deep in his chest.

This was almost too much for Jeb, who felt he was about to wet his breeches. The ghost was talking out loud to old Miz Manning as if she were a youngster. He honestly thought he might faint.

"Jebediah, this is George Raven's Wing, a member of the Crow Indian tribe. It is his Grandfather whose spirit haunts the cistern."

The man turned toward him with an intense, black-eyed stare which Jeb felt to his core, and made him sure his knees were going to fail him just like the rest of his body had.

"George, this is Jebediah Jenkins, who is a great help to me in the garden," Mrs. Manning said politely.

Up close, it was obvious that the man bore all the distinguishing traits of a Native American. It was also apparent that he was extremely old. His entire face, including the prominent, high cheek bones and hawkish nose, were deeply wrinkled, naturally bronze, and deepened to a copper color by the sun. His silver gray hair was pulled back in a long, single braid, which fell almost to his waist. He was dressed in snake skin boots, very old weathered jeans, and a light-colored buckskin jacket. A rolled bandanna was tied across his forehead. From the ties hung three black, iridescent feathers which lay glistening upon one shoulder.

He nodded briefly, acknowledging Jeb. "Jebediah." The name rumbled up from within him. Then he turned again to Mrs. Manning. The deep timbered voice spoke. "You have fared well, Friend." It was not a question but an appraisal; and she bowed her head in accepting his compliment. "You also, Friend." She stated.

With these amenities completed, the man turned and strode off down the hill and out of sight.

Jeb was still stunned. His knees gave out and he sank to the ground where he was. He didn't see the slight grin that deepened the creases around Mrs. Manning's mouth and eyes as she turned toward the house. His gaze wouldn't leave the sight of the departing Indian.

"Come up on the porch, please, Jebediah. I'll bring out something to drink. I know you've had the shock of your life, and working after that might present quite a problem. Besides, I also know your curiosity is working overtime. Maybe today is the propitious time for the rest of the story."

Jeb didn't even so much as think of his dictionary. He was too flabbergasted. Even if his voice still didn't work just right, his mind did. His only thought at that moment was *Lord, be praised!*

 Chapter Eight

Peach season was at its height. The succulent fruit was on the market everywhere; and Mrs. Manning had a peach tree at the side of the yard across from the vegetable garden. Jeb could smell the luscious aroma of the sweet, ripe flesh from where he was weeding the tomatoes.

Lord, how he disliked this weeding business, and even worse were the big, fat green and black tomato bugs. He hadn't done this particular job for about a week and was shocked to see two of the tomato plants almost bare of leaves and sporting those awful worms which he had to search for to pull off. Their coloring and the way they curled up against the leaves was such an effective camouflage it made them the dickens to find. The fat old worms were so squirmy, and when you stepped on them they shot out that terrible green, squishy stuff they had been devouring and digesting from the plants. Killing those blasted pests was not one of his favorite pastimes, but it was a "yucky" chore which had to be done to save the tomatoes. Miz Manning wasn't much for chemical sprays on her vegetables.

Daisy loved to watch the wiggly things and paw at them. Jeb had a heck of a time keeping her out from under his feet and away from the slimy green mess they made.

Jeb put all the weeds in a pile and decided to take a break for lunch. It was Saturday and he planned to work through most of the day, so he had brought a sack lunch his mother made for him, and of course, his usual can of Pepsi. The weather was hot but not blistery, with a dancy little breeze to temper it a bit.

He decided to sit in the shade under the peach tree and eat because he could look over most of the yard and take a kind of inventory for everything that needed to be done.

One of the things Jeb found most intriguing about Mrs. Manning's garden was, never, so far in all the months he had worked here, was there a time when something wasn't blooming. She had told him about all the flowers that came up from the bulbs. After their blooming season they just petered out and went dormant, Mrs. Manning said.

He was sorely disappointed when his beloved Pansies, not planted from bulbs, went so tiny and finally gave up the fight. He was told that Pansies were hardly little flowers and didn't mind the cooler weather of the early spring, as long as there wasn't a hard frost. It was the really hot days that seemed to do them in. Then they turned wild and rangy, became sickly yellow-green, wilted and died. Pansy plants had to be set in again early every year because, Jeb learned, they were annuals, not perennials. Well, he didn't think he'd mind so much planting those little buggers again because he thought so much of them.

When he first came here, there were lots of flowers blooming their heads off; but now, with the consistent hotter summer weather, there were even more. Over in a bed that got some sun and partial shade were what Mrs. Manning called Impatiens. Those colorful little things couldn't seem to bud and flower fast enough to suit themselves. They doubled and tripled in size, too, and sort of took over the space where you put them.

The edges of most of the beds were showing off also. They sported bouquet on bouquet and row after row of Alyssum. "Carpet of Snow", Mrs. Manning said they were popularly called, and they were just that. The hotter the weather, the more they spread out and grew together in clumps. They were a very "white" white and sprawled all over the place, overgrowing their beds and cascading down over the rocks that formed the borders like little flower falls. Jeb dubbed them spectacular. There was purple Alyssum, too, mighty pretty, but he thought the white ones outdid them by a mile.

Mrs. Manning was right funny about the way she named all the flowers as if they were elegant old friends. She never just said they were red or pink or blue. Oh, no! She always called them kinda sophisticated color names that Jeb had to hunt up in the dictionary. So he could have a chance to learn, she would designate them by their horticultural names; but then she would say they were scarlet or crimson, ruby, garnet, vermillion, magenta, azure and shocking pink.

Jeb thought it was a kind of quaint way she had of showing her affection and enjoyment of them.

Down by the rocks, Miz Manning had a bed of Four O'Clocks. Jeb thought that was a real crazy name for any kind of flower. But they were true to what they were called, and wouldn't open their pretty red trumpet-shaped faces until late afternoon.

His eye fell on the sun dial, and his thought zoomed to that scary time when Mr. George Raven's Wing had come for his seasonal visit. Jeb didn't like to dwell on it because he had been frightened out of his wits and was even now a whole lot embarrassed by that event. But when he finally got his breath and his legs back, he and Mrs. Manning had sat on the porch, and she related the entire story of the haunted cistern that day.

He had finished his sandwich and was just starting to eat the fresh peach his mother had packed for him when Gaddy Taylor came out of the house with a plate of cookies she'd made.

Mrs. Taylor was a short, outspoken Black woman who was about as wide as she was tall. She came once a week to keep house for Mrs. Manning, just as Jeb's mother had once done. Sometimes she came to serve when Mrs. Manning had a dinner party. Jeb didn't know whether to love her or hate her.

Once in a while she seemed to boss him around like she owned the place. "Jeb, Miz Manning say for you to work in the vegetable garden today while she gone out, so get to it, boy!" The next thing he knew, she'd be bringing him out something delicious she had baked, like the cookies today, as if she was trying to make up for being bossy. Sometimes she was a right jolly person, but more than often she got herself in a snit, and if Mrs. Manning was away, Jeb seemed to take the brunt of it. Gaddy handed him the cookies, but now she was looking at him askance.

"What right you got to be eating Miz Manning's peaches, boy?"

Jeb felt his spine go rigid. "This isn't Miz Manning's peach, Miz Taylor. I brought it in my lunch," Jeb said cautiously.

"Uh huh!" she said, looking pointedly at the tempting, ripe fruit hanging from the tree above him. "That's a likely story. You sitting under her peach tree eating a peach, right?" She scurried back into the house.

What she'd implied really riled Jeb and he was sorely put out, but he didn't move and kept on eating his peach.

Moments later, Mrs. Manning came out and walked casually over to where he was sitting. He could tell by the look on her face that Gaddy had "told" on him. He stood up politely and waited for what he suspected was coming.

"Jebediah, are you enjoying the peach?" she said off-handedly. "Yessum," Jeb replied honestly. "Well, Jebediah, you are welcome to a peach or a tomato or anything else from the garden. I just wish you would ask permission first."

Jeb couldn't really believe what he was hearing. He thought Miz Manning trusted him, wouldn't think twice about what Miz Taylor had said. He was deeply crushed to think she didn't believe him. He took a deep breath because it was hard for him to speak. "This is my peach, Miz Manning. I brought it with me in my lunch sack."

"Oh?" she questioned, her eyebrows raised. Jeb became very still. They stared at each other for a few seconds that seemed to drag on forever. Then Jeb stooped to retrieve his brown paper lunch sack, put the remainder of the peach in it and said very slowly, "Yessum, it is. Whether you believe me or not. I'm not lying!" With that, he started walking down the driveway, much in the manner George Raven's Wing strode away.

"Well!!" exclaimed Mrs. Manning to herself after he had gone, "He's certainly got his dander up." She glanced over to the spot where he had been sitting under the peach tree. He had left the plate of cookies untouched. "After all, evidence is evidence, even if it is circumstantial."

Then she began to think of the shy, willing young man she had come to like so much; of his quick mind and sense of humor. *If I have misjudged him*, she thought, *I have made a terrible mistake.*

Chapter Nine

Jeb was so furious that walking home had been a real ordeal for the first time. In his anger and disappointment, his feet dragged as if they were slogging through wet cement. He simply couldn't understand why Miz Manning had lost faith in him and didn't trust him. He felt utterly betrayed. He mumbled to himself every step of the way as he trudged along.

How could she be so dumb as to believe there was a ghost in that stupid cistern and not believe him? He was flesh and blood and he did not lie! His folks had been very clear with all the family on that subject.

That daggone Gaddy Taylor, old busybody, got Miz Manning all ruffled up, and what for? For nothing! That's what! Except now I'm in deep trouble and it's not my fault. Those two old biddies got burrs up their butts... He stopped dead in his tracks. Jeb knew his Momma would like to whale the daylights outta him for just thinking like that. No that she ever would, but she sure would give it a good think.

"Shape up, Jeb. Get a grip! You got to think on this thing some and find a way to prove yourself, man!" he admonished himself.

When he got home he had to tell his mother why he was home so early. She was aghast that Mrs. Manning would think so little of him. Laticia tried her best to comfort him. She knew how deeply he was hurt.

"Son, sometimes things really don't turn out fair. Once in a while good people get blamed for things they didn't do. Every now and again life's like that, even if we don't understand it and know it's not just," she consoled. "I could go talk to her for you, Jeb. I might be able to straighten things out."

"No, Momma. Don't do that. Please don't you do that. This here is something I got to handle by myself if I'm ever fixing to grow up. Thank you for wanting to help, but I just got to do it alone."

Jeb's mother ached for his battered feelings but she was proud of his decision.

That night at the dinner table, Jeb was the only quiet one. Laticia understood what was bothering him, so she tried to keep the conversation light. The main topic lately had been the supposed ghost in the cistern and the day Jeb had seen George Raven's Wing. When Jeb had come home and related the events of the afternoon, the sight of the old Indian chanting on the sun dial, and the story Mrs. Manning told him later, he was still mighty shaken. His appetite hadn't been his usual teenage boy ravenous that night.

The whole family had been wide-eyed at the whopping tale.

After the jolt he got that day, he and Mrs. Manning had sat on the porch for a long time while he tried to get his equilibrium back. Daisy was still hiding in the shrubbery where she had been ever since the old Indian made his appearance.

Mrs. Manning told him that when she and her husband first purchased the acreage on which they were to build their home, they had a visit from George Raven's Wing.

Many people around Valleyville knew about the local Indian. Many of the Crow, a Sioux-speaking tribe of the Plains Indians, had migrated northwest to eastern Montana when the white settlers came in numbers to the Kansas Territory. But some of them, at that time, having begun a rudimentary type of farming and a fairly profitable business trade with the White men, stayed to live in a small colony approximately thirty miles north of Valleyville.

For reasons of his own, George Raven's Wing didn't live among them. He resided down by the river. Every other year or so the river would flood and he would take his tools and a few belongings and live temporarily among other flood victims on the gym floor of the Valleyville Municipal Building. When the water receded, George would return to the shack, clean out, and resume his life as if nothing had happened.

He was a wood carver and crafted small figures of animals from the driftwood he found along the banks of the river. These he sold from time to time to help sustain himself. He worked at other odd jobs around the town, but otherwise kept pretty much to himself.

Folks thought of him as an oddity and suspected he was a little addled in the head. Some people knew about the ghost legend, but no one put much stock in it.

When George Raven's Wing first visited the Mannings, Mrs. Manning said they were a bit leery of him and didn't know quite what to think.

He regaled them with a fascinating story which began in the 1870s, after the Civil War when many more White people began migrating to the west. George's grandfather, Black Feather, had been about twenty-five years old at the time. He was married to a beautiful Indian woman. They had a young baby boy about a year old. One night, when they were traveling to their people north of Valleyville, which was then only a small community, they had stopped at the cistern to get fresh water for the rest of their journey.

Camped near the cistern was a White man, probably an outlaw, drunked up on rot-gut whiskey, who took a fancy to the Crow's pretty Indian wife. Black Feather had fought desperately with the man, who drew his gun, shot, and killed the Indian, and threw his body into the cistern. His wife had fled into the night with their child to escape the murdering renegade. Black Feather's wife and the babe eventually made it to the tribe's village with the news of the terrible happening. The child, of course, was George Raven's Wing's father, Raven.

But it was not only George's Grandmother who kept the story alive. Word began to circulate throughout nearby towns that the cistern was haunted by the ghost of an Indian. Eventually, word of this tale reached the tribe in the north.

This particular cistern was marked on maps the settlers carried with them, showing where they could get supplies of fresh water. Many of the travelers reported they were unable to get water there because a ghost was guarding the cistern. The story goes that several folks swore as they prepared to bring up water, a specter rose from the reservoir and frightened them so badly they ran away.

The Crow tribe believed that Black Feather was protecting people from taking the water that had been contaminated by his decaying body. The legend grew until no one stopped for water there anymore.

Mrs. Manning said George told them he had heard the story all his young life, from his Grandmother, from his mother, and from the tribal members, who told the tale repeatedly around their home fires. He realized that his Grandfather was a hero to his people, and that his soul was still not free to enter the spirit world. This fact had greatly upset him from the beginning, when he was old enough to understand the legend.

When he came of age, George journeyed to Valleyville to dwell close to where his Grandfather remained, and pray for the peace of his spirit. He came to the cistern in every season to appeal to the Great Father on behalf of Black Feather's soul.

Mrs. Manning told Jeb that no matter what she and Mr. Manning thought about the matter, they both resolved to honor George Raven's Wing's quest. That's when her husband had decided to close up the cistern and had the heavy sun dial made to protect the site. This show of faith had endeared them to George, who had respected their property in return and became their life-long friend.

George Raven's Wing was now ninety-seven years old.

Mrs. Manning said that in all the years she and her husband had lived there, they had never seen anything untoward. But several people who knew about the lore had sworn to them that, in driving by on a moonlit night, they had seen what appeared to be a misty aura, clearly human in form, hovering above the sun dial.

Jeb's eyes almost popped out when she told him that. *Lord have mercy!* he thought in a panic, *I'm making up my mind right here and now never to go near Miz Manning's house on a night when the moon is up.*

Chapter Ten

The unfortunate peach episode happened on Saturday. Jeb had wrestled all weekend with the problem of how to explain the situation to her, and get back in Mrs. Manning's good graces. Finally in the middle of the night, as he sleeplessly tossed and turned, an idea had come to him. Something he had seen when he accidentally stepped on a rotting peach under that tree made him feel he had the answer. He was sure it would be the only way to prove himself.

Monday he went to work in the garden as usual when he had finished at the newspaper and carried his lunch with him.

Mrs. Manning came out onto the porch and looked down at him. He was sitting under her peach tree calmly eating a peach. Casually she walked down the porch steps and stopped in front of him. Daisy followed her out of the house and stepped onto Jeb's leg, kneading his jeans and sniffing at the peach.

"You left in such a huff the other day, Jebediah, I am surprised to see you back for work again." Slowly Jeb placed the cat on the ground and stood up politely, but said nothing.

"Is this defiance, perhaps, Jebediah? The acid test? Or are you trying to prove something to me?"

Without answering directly, he took something from his paper lunch sack and held out his hand to her. Within his palm lay the shriveled, brown remains of a half-eaten peach.

"See this here, Miz Manning? This here's the peach I was eating Saturday when you and Miz Taylor thought I had taken it from your tree." He held out the other hand in which lay the partially consumed peach he had begun munching on. "This here's the peach I was just now eating." He paused for effect. "You said I might take one of your peaches if I asked your permission?" Mrs. Manning nodded. "Well, I'm asking now. Please, can I have one of your peaches?"

She knew he was testing her, and that the logic of it was in his mind, so she said calmly, "Yes, you may."

Jeb stepped from under the small tree and began to look over the ripe fruit. He took his time in selecting a large, juicy peach and picked it carefully from the limb. He wiped it gently on his trouser leg and took a big bite from it, then another, right down to the pit. He chewed thoughtfully, looking straight as Mrs. Manning all the while. She didn't know whether to be amused or irritated; but she felt the moment was of great significance to him so she waited patiently.

"Miz Manning," Jeb said solemnly, "See these two peaches I told you I brought with me for my lunch?" Again she nodded. "Now, look here at your peach. My peaches that Momma bought at the Valleyville Super Mart are cling peaches. Yours is a freestone peach. The reason I know this is because one day I accidentally stepped on a rotten peach that dropped under the tree and the seed popped right out. Now, do you see I wasn't taking your peaches?"

The look on Mrs. Manning's face was inscrutable, but as she stared at the fruit he held, a sadness came into her eyes. "Jebediah, I have done you a great wrong. I am sorry. Please, forgive me." She turned abruptly and walked stiffly back into the house.

A disgruntled cat, having been dismissed without the usual affection she expected, twined around his legs mewling pitifully. Jeb picked her up, still staring at the house where Mrs. Manning had gone in. He hugged Daisy to him and rubbed her ears and chin, which brought about an instant, grateful cat motor.

Mrs. Manning's reaction puzzled Jeb. He didn't know what he was supposed to do now. He just hoped he was somewhat vindicated. He went ahead and did the work he had come to do and left for home.

Right before suppertime the doorbell rang at Jeb's house. He was the closest to it, so he opened the door. Mrs. Manning stood on his front stoop holding a freshly-baked pie. He was so surprised he couldn't speak.

"Jebediah, this is my offering of humble pie. It's better than eating crow." He hadn't the slightest idea what she was talking about and the look on his face told her so.

"I baked you a peach pie," she explained. "It's my humble apology to you. I shall never doubt you again, Jebediah. That's a promise!"

A huge smile broke out on Jeb's face as he took the pie she proffered.

"Friends?" she asked and stuck out her hand.

"Yessum," relief washed over Jeb as, still smiling, he took her hand. "Friends!"

# *Chapter Eleven*

Jeb returned to school in September for his Junior year. He only went to Mrs. Manning's house two afternoons a week and sometimes on Saturday for a few hours.

There was plenty to do in the yard during the fall, but not nearly as much work in the flower beds as before. They still had raking leaves ahead of them. Lord knows there was bound to be humongous amounts of leaves with all those big, old trees. She said the roses and some of the other plants would have to be mulched; and there would be lots of pruning to do so the trees and shrubs wouldn't overgrow in the spring.

She asked him if he knew any other nice boys at school who would be willing to come from time to time to help with some of the heavier work, since it was so time consuming and too much for just the two of them. He told her he would try to find someone.

Jeb thought there might be one or two guys at school, his friend Billy, maybe, and somebody at the newspaper who might like the work for a little extra money, especially outdoors.

Jeb still worked at the paper after school the other days of the week because he really felt he and his family needed the money, and he liked that work, too. Working for the Manning family was a right good deal. They expected you to work hard and to be dependable; but the pay was fair and they treated everybody pretty nice from what he could tell.

When Mrs. Manning paid him, she did so by personal check written out to him. She asked him to keep track of his hours, and he knew she kept track, too. Sometimes he would tell her how long he had worked and she would remind him of some extra time he had forgotten or overlooked. When he got the money it was usually right on the dime. Once in a while, if there had been a very difficult job, longer hours, or even a bit of hard labor, she would include a little bonus. That really tickled Jeb, and he always made sure to thank her kindly. He thought that pleased her also.

The air grew chilly and crisp. Jeb loved the weather like that because a body didn't work up such a sweat doing heavy work outside and the brisk days seemed to fill him with more energy.

He got Billy Jones, his friend from history class, to come with him two afternoons a week. That helped a lot, and Mrs. Manning took to Billy right away because he was polite, if a little shy, and could do the work real well. Daisy allowed Billy to pet her but she didn't pester him like she did Jeb. Secretly, Jeb was very pleased by this seeming preference.

He also got Hack Slater, his neighbor down the street, to come on Saturdays, sometimes even when Jeb wasn't there. Hack was a little older. Jeb felt sorry for him because he had dropped out of school a while back and couldn't seem to get a job. Mrs. Manning accepted Hack but Jeb could tell she didn't care for him very much. He was fairly outspoken, cocky, sort of, and walked with a swagger that kind of rubbed against Mrs. Manning's grain. The cat treated Hack with arrogance and disdain and never went anywhere near him. Obviously, no approval there from the "manager", Jeb thought. It was just as well because Hack said he couldn't stand cats. Belatedly, Jeb remembered that Hack was the one who had lured him and Eli into that big batch of trouble a while back; and he hoped he hadn't made a mistake in asking him.

The first day Hack came to work he seemed to be polite enough. But when Mrs. Manning asked him to do some heavy tree trimming, he rolled his eyes and gave her a sour look and replied, "Okay, Lady, if you say so."

Mrs. Manning's eyebrows shot up. "Young man, my name is Mrs. Manning, and I'd thank you to remember that in the future." She turned her back and practically huffed off into the house. The boys all stared after her in disbelief at this unusual display of temper.

Hack began to mumble under his breath as he strode off to the garage to get the trimmer. It was a good thing Jeb and Billy couldn't hear the words clearly. They would have been shocked.

Lord, Jeb thought, *no wonder he can't get a job if he acts like that all the time.*

"I guess I better talk to Hack and tell him it's sorta different up here at Miz Manning's. We all ought to mind our manners. She's an old lady and, after all, she is paying us for the job we do."

"What's eating him this time?" Billy was raking leaves next to the flower bed Jeb was mulching.

"Beats me," Jeb paused to look after Hack. "Seems like he got out on the wrong side of the bed this morning."

"Might say that any day about Hack," Billy whispered. Both boys snickered and went on with their work.

Oh, Mrs. Manning was nice enough to both Billy and Hack, but after that first day when she and Hack had that sort of falling out, she avoided speaking directly to Hack whenever possible. She would let Jeb tell them the areas that needed work and specifically what she wanted done.

Jeb didn't blame her for not wanting to tangle with anymore of Hack's lip. In fact, he felt a little guilty that there was a problem at all. But he kind of liked being in charge, like a straw boss. Anyway, he'd been here longer than they had and knew the ropes pretty good. He noticed that Mrs. Manning never had cookies or drinks when the other boys worked there with him.

Mrs. Manning's longtime friend, Harry Bains, had a hauling business. He and his son, Daryll, brought a truck over every week or so to take away the pruned tree branches and take off the extra leaves that didn't get to the "heap". They had been helping Mrs. Manning with that kind of work since Harry first started up the business many years ago. Daryll had been only a little tyke when his father first began letting him come along.

Finally, most of the heavy work was finished for the season. All they could do at any rate.

"Well, I guess you won't be around for a while, Jebediah," Mrs. Manning said, sadly. "I'll miss seeing you. I'm proud of your work and how much you have learned."

They were sitting on the porch again, bundled up for a chilly fall day. Both of them were reluctant to say a final winter good-bye to each other. Mrs. Manning had fixed them hot spiced apple juice in token of the crisp weather. Jeb thought it tasted some kind of good.

"Now, don't forget, in the spring, I intend to take up where we left off. Is it a deal?" she asked hopefully.

Jeb grinned, agreed, and shook her hand. Soon after that the snow began to fly. It was nearly Thanksgiving. There would be a few days off from school, but after that just getting to school through the slush of ice and snow would be a hassle. He wasn't looking forward to it.

# *Chapter Twelve*

Jeb was surprised at how much he missed working with Mrs. Manning. They had a right peculiar kind of friendship going, that old lady and him, he acknowledged. He did go up to the house every two weeks or so to turn over that rotting mound Mrs. Manning put so much store in. She was usually gone, though, off to play bridge with her "girls" or to do some work with her church ladies as she often did. Sometimes when she was home, she would step out on the porch for a minute and wave to him; but it was too cold for visiting long.

Every now and then, if it was her day to work at Mrs. Manning's, Gaddy would stick her head out the back door and yell a greeting. She might even tell him to stop by before he left because she was baking something delicious, and she'd offer him a bite.

One very cold day in mid-winter, Jeb had just finished turning over the compost pile. He was putting the shovel in the garage and ready to start for home, when he heard the familiar, eerie chanting. Chilled though he already was, he froze on the spot and looked down the hill toward the cistern.

George Raven's Wing stood with his arms in the air, his weathered face turned to the gray winter sky. He looked much the same as Jeb had remembered him that first dreadful time.

He was wearing very similar clothes to those he had worn in the heat of summer. It was as if the intensity of his mind-set made him impervious to the bitter cold.

As if sensing that someone was watching him, George lowered his arms and turned to look up at Jeb. Jeb felt like ducking into the garage but knew that was a cowardly thing to do, and the sight of the old Indian seemed to hypnotize him. Once again his body remained immobile.

George waved his arm in a salute of recognition and then strode away down to the street.

Jeb returned the wave automatically, but dropped his hand in relief and took a deep breath to get a hold on himself. He decided to walk home slowly in spite of the cold, though he didn't think he would catch up the old man considering how big his steps were and how fast he walked. He knew in his mind Mr. Raven's Wing wasn't the ghost. But just being around him kind of gave Jeb the creeps and he didn't want to take any chances.

At least the old compost mess hadn't seemed to smell quite so bad in the icy air. Lord, that was a relief!

Close to Christmas, Mrs. Manning showed up at his house early one evening. She and his mother greeted each other like it was old home week. Kind of embarrassed him a little to see two grown women talking on so, just because they hadn't seen each other in a long time.

She had brought a bunch of stuff for his family; a box of her spiced, sugared pecans she said she was famous for, some homemade cookies, and cranberry sauce. His mother handed around the pecans and all the family tasted one or two. *Pretty good*, he thought. But then everything Mrs. Manning made that he had tasted so far was mighty fine.

His mother plunked the lid back on the pecan box and whisked it away so they wouldn't eat such a special treat all at once...and the cookies with them. Momma said the cranberry sauce would go real good with the turkey Mister Carter had given each of the employees at the paper.

After all the greetings, tasting, and small talk died down a little, Mrs. Manning pulled a brightly-wrapped package out of the box she had brought.

"This is for you, Jebediah. You may open it any time you wish. It's a gift for you to enjoy every day. I just chose to give it to you now."

Jeb was speechless. It was heavy and he couldn't think what in the world it might be. The fact that she had given him a personal gift stunned him and he was very embarrassed that he had nothing for her. He didn't know exactly what to do or say. Just "thank you" didn't seem like quite enough.

"That's mighty nice of you, Miz Manning," he stated hesitantly. "I truly do appreciate it. You want me to open it now?"

"It's up to you, Jebediah."

He sort of suspicioned she wanted him to open it so she could see whether he liked it or not. Besides, his curiosity had a right tight hold on him. He looked at his mother who nodded, so he began to tear at the wrapping. Jeb had to elbow his little sister, Naomi, out of the way to get a good look at the gift. It was a large book. He read the title: A COMPLETE PICTORIAL THESAURUS OF GROWING THINGS

At first he didn't quite understand what it meant. But he began to leaf through the pages and saw the bright colors jump out at him. He recognized some of the flowers and shrubs he had been working with all year long, and a wide grin creased his face.

"I hope you like it and will enjoy it for a long time, Jebediah." Mrs. Manning smiled happily at him.

"Oh, yessum, I surely do like it, I surely do, and thank you, Miz Manning, thank you very much."

At the time, Jeb wracked his brain trying to think of something he could give Mrs. Manning. Nothing set just right with him, or if something seemed a fitting gift, he didn't have enough money to buy it. So he settled on sending her a nice Christmas card.

He went to the store that carried a line of the best greeting cards, and searched for an hour until he found what he thought was the perfect one. One with lots of growing things; Poinsettias, Holly, Mistletoe, and Pine. The sentiment read: WISHING A BLESSED HOLIDAY SEASON TO A VERY SPECIAL PERSON. He wrote at the bottom of the card; Merry Christmas to Mrs. Manning from Jebediah Jenkins. Thanks again for the book. I like it a lot.

It would have pleased and surprised him to know that his card had brought tears to Mrs. Manning's eyes, and that she had put it away for safe keeping in her souvenir box.

Chapter Thirteen

Jeb read from his book every night. His brothers teased him about it but he didn't mind all that much. When he read about the plants and shrubs he had worked with, he found that Mrs. Manning was right on the money with all her instructions to him. He read about other plants he was not familiar with but which caught his interest. He wondered if Mrs. Manning might be interested also if he told her about some of them next spring.

Somehow, his grades at school began to improve just a bit. He was sure happy about that, and he reckoned it might have something to do with all that reading he'd been doing. Maybe, maybe not.

That winter was cold and bitter and he began to worry about the roses and some of the other plants. Would they lose a few of them because of the cold? Did they put as much mulch as needed on everything to keep it warm and protected enough?

"Fussy old woman!" he grunched under his breath. "Forget about all that stuff. Go to a basketball game. Have some fun for a change," he chided himself.

Most times he and Billy or Jerry, or even once in a while Eli, did go to the game and cheered their team as loudly and faithfully as their schoolmates. And he did hang out with all the other guys from class he knew. Fact was, he had his eye on a new girl in his home room, Cordelia Kidd.

She was a looker, all right. Big, shiny, chestnut brown eyes and pretty teeth. She made friends real quick and was popular with a lot of people, including the teachers. He tried every chance he got, without being too obvious, to sit by her at the ball games; and she seemed mighty nice. He expected, though, that by the time he got up his nerve to ask her out, one of the team guys would have snagged her interest.

Cordelia Kidd had come to the Valleyville High School for the second semester. Her father served in the military and had been transferred from Fort Leonard Wood in Missouri to the Army Post near Valleyville. Jeb had been fascinated to hear her talking with her girl friends and sometimes in class, about how she had lived with her family on military posts in Germany and Japan. She new things about the world and people and had seen places that Jeb had never dreamed existed. This fact made her seem rather exotic somehow in Jeb's mind.

Her father was a career man, a Staff Sergeant, held in great esteem by his men. Cordelia's mother worked as a volunteer with the American Red Cross and taught Sunday school at their church. Her brother, Colin, was ten years old. She brought him with her to some of the games. Jeb had discovered he was a real, genuine, pain-in-the-neck-pest! Worse than Naomi!

Jeb supposed that having been in several countries all over the world, and having moved from place to place every few years, were the reasons Cordelia was so good around all kinds of people and why she made friends so easily.

Anyways, he knew he had a hankering for her, more than any other girl he'd ever known. The only thing that stumped him was he really didn't know enough about girls to know how to go about attracting her. Because he thought so much of her, he despised being overcome by shyness and by his inexperience when it came to knowing anything about women.

He would have been dumfounded and super pleased if he had known that, secretly, Cordelia also had her eye on him. She saw something real and fine in the plain, shy boy who kept sitting by her at all the games. He seemed so different and more appealing than all the boys who were coming on to her strong and cocky-like. They mostly reminded her of Banty roosters, strutting and full of themselves rushing her. It scared her a little, even if it was kind of flattering. She really did like Jeb, though; but she thought it wouldn't look "cool" if she let him know that too soon.

The winter hadn't been quite as severe as Kansas winters have a tendency to be. Jeb was grateful for that. Besides school and his work at the newspaper, Jeb did all the things any normal boy would do to have a good time. But frequently, he would stop and think about Mrs. Manning's garden. Sometimes his mind was there even when he wasn't. His thoughts of all those growing things drew him like a magnet, especially when he was reading those books she had given him.

The season was about to get sprung and he was fixing to bust a gasket to get back there.

# Chapter Fourteen

The very end of March had just about blown itself to a frazzle and seemed to be taming down a whole lot to let go for April. It was a beautiful, sunny afternoon, a fragile, early spring warm-up. Signs of the new season appeared to be everywhere, even in Jeb's jaunty step when he strode up the driveway to Mrs. Manning's house.

As he walked, he began to assess any damage he felt winter might have come down with. The grass was starting to green up under the dead brown top layer. Some bare spots showed here and there. *Might need some reseeding*, he speculated. A cluster of native Cedar trees looked pretty "burned" from the cold. He wondered if they would right themselves presently or if they would need more pruning or a bit of fertilizing help. He'd have to ask Mrs. Manning. He was pretty sure she would know what they ought to do. He tried not to even look at the sun dial.

Around the rocks and trees, Crocus' were blooming, and some of the Hyacinths, Jonquils, and Tulips they had labored so long to replant were poking out a little spotty color, ready to come out full blast.

Before he was halfway up to the house, Mrs. Manning came out the back door and hailed him from the porch. *She must have been watching out for me from the kitchen window*, he thought. That notion pleased him.

"Hello, Jebediah," she called. "Happy spring!"

He jogged the rest of the way to greet her, and smiled his biggest smile when she took both his hands in hers and squeezed hard. "I'm so glad to see you, Jebediah. I've really missed you."

"Yessum," he grinned. "Me, too."

She looked him over, assessing him from the winter also. "Why, Jebediah, I do believe you've grown another foot," she declared. He glanced at his shoes and then stated with a straight face, "No Ma'am, I still got only two."

Mrs. Manning threw up her hands laughing and enjoying the joke. "You've grown quite a sense of humor, too, haven't you, young man?" Jeb just grinned. He liked having spoofed her a little.

Daisy bounded around the corner of the house and practically attacked the legs of his jeans, rubbing, purring loudly, and meowing in greeting. He picked her up, causing her motor to kick into a high gear. Jeb hugged the big cat and smiled. He hadn't realized how much he had missed her, too.

"Come with me, Jebediah, I've got something to show you." He tagged along until he saw the direction she was heading. Lord, she was going directly for that danged "heap".

"Look here, our magic elixir has completed processing and it's ready to do more good work." Daisy jumped out of his arms and dashed back toward the house.

He lagged back a little waiting for the malodorous blast to hit him, and he watched mesmerized as she stuck her gloved hand into the gunk. Jeb was surprised to see that small, uniform particles sifted down through her fingers. He sniffed warily. Then he sniffed again. When he sniffed real hard, he smelled the aroma of soil, a little strong, but not unpleasant. *Well, I'll be dadburned*, he thought. *She was right on the money again.* He should have known.

"This is ready to put on the vegetable garden. You and Billy and Hack can dig it up and work in this wonderful compost next Saturday, if you will. Then we can get a head start on planting some of the hardier things like spinach."

Oh Lord, spinach again already! Jeb's stomached flinched at the thought.

To get her off the spinach track for a minute, Jeb said, "Miz Manning, I've been reading up this past winter in that book you gave me, and I saw a few things that you don't have in the yard that might be real pretty, if you'd be willing to try."

Intrigued, Mrs. Manning asked what exactly he had in mind. "Well, I've been reading about Azaleas."

"Azaleas! Azaleas are beautiful, Jebediah, but they wouldn't weather through winter in this Kansas climate."

"Now, I know that's the usual way of things, Miz Manning, but the book says they've come out with some hardy new hy...hyber..."

"Hybrids?" she encouraged.

"Yessum, that's them, hybrids. They say if you get some of these stronger plants and plant 'em in a sheltered place and mulch 'em good, they'd probably do just fine."

Mrs. Manning stared at Jeb for quite some time as if she were mulling over his proposition. "I'm proud of you, Jebediah. It's apparent you've been doing in-depth perusal of that book I gave you, and a good deal of analytical thinking."

Lord, he'd forgotten to bring his dictionary with him this time.

"Just where would you suggest we put these hybrid Azaleas, if we decided to get some, Jebediah?"

"I've been thinking right much on that question. Follow 'round here to the porch side and I'll show you."

The garage was set out farther than the house on the north and created a protected L-shape back to the porch. Jeb explained that the small bedding plants, creeping Phlox, Star of Bethlehem, and Grape Hyacinths didn't show off much against the house because they were so low to the ground. He proposed that they be moved out to front some of the other beds of annuals and that the Azaleas be planted against the side of the garage wall for a show of color there, as well as for protection.

Mrs. Manning walked slowly up and down in front of the garage wall, pondering and muttering to herself. Jeb held his breath, waiting. Maybe he'd overstepped himself a mite. Lord, he hoped not!

"Jebediah, you're a genius. That's quite a good idea, and I think it just might work. Azaleas would be gorgeous there. In fact, I can hardly wait to try it. Get in the car. I'm going in to get my purse and my keys, and we'll go right now and see if Dalgren's Nursery has any of these special plants."

She picked up the cat and took her into the house when she went to get her purse. She returned in what seemed to Jeb like record time.

Miz Manning at the wheel again! Heaven help us! Jeb agonized. Her old Cadillac was long as a boat and wide as a tank. Merely maneuvering that thing was a test of skill. He held on for dear life as they made the ski jump start at the top of the drive. The abrupt stop at the bottom of the hill made him feel like he was going out through the windshield. Jeb was mighty grateful he had fastened his seatbelt and pulled it tight. *Lord be praised, we made it!* he thought for what seemed the hundredth time as they merged slowly into the traffic.

They arrived at Dalgren's Nursery, all right, but Jeb had kept his eyes closed most of the way. It hadn't been too bad. They only ran over one curbing, but his worst moment had come when they coasted slowly through a yellow warning light at a busy intersection. Mrs. Manning had remained unperturbed, but Jeb found it very rewarding to feel solid ground under his feet.

This was the first time Jeb had been to the nursery and as he looked around, the feast that met his eyes stunned him. Flowers were blooming everywhere. There were planted in beds, in every kind and size of planter, and even hanging in pots suspended from the porch roof of the small building that fronted a line of glass greenhouses. There were flowering shrubs of every size and color; evergreen shrubs and many varieties of young trees. Peat pots of tea roses, floribunda and climbers, not yet ready for blooming, were sporting large, brilliant-colored tags proclaiming their promised beauty. He was simply awed by the sight. He loved it!

Felix Dalgren rushed out the door to greet them, a huge, blustery man with rosy cheeks and hands like bunches of bananas. Noisy and robust, he was the least likely prototype of a nurseryman. He was also a man who loved his vocation, and was adored by his customers.

"Mandy Lil! Welcome! Now, I know it's officially spring whenever I see your pretty face," he boomed. Jeb peeked at Mrs. Manning to see how she was taking such an enthusiastic and familiar greeting, and was amazed to see that she was blushing.

"Go on with you, Felix, you flattering buffoon. I've known you since you were knee-high to a duck. You like to make over me so much because I've bought enough plants from you all these years to add three new rooms to your house." Both of them tilted back their heads and shared a hardy laugh. Jeb was tremendously amused by this bantering exchange.

"Felix, this is Jebediah Jenkins, who helps me with my yard.

We're here to do some serious business. We want to try some hybrid Azaleas."

"Hello there, young man. Glad to make your acquaintance," bellowed Mr. Dalgren, as he vigorously shook Jeb's hand.

"Now, you surprise me, Mandy Lil. A few of your gardening friends have already got the jump on you there, trying out some Azaleas, and having pretty good success with them, too." Felix chuckled and led them into one of the greenhouses.

Felix Dalgren and his wife Beulah had immigrated to North America with their families from Norway when they were small children. At first they had lived in Ontario, Canada. But other friends of their families had settled in the United States, in Kansas, so their parents eventually moved here to be closer to people they had known from "back home". Their two families had always lived near one another and Beulah and Felix had known each other all their young lives. It seemed fitting that they should fall in love and marry when they were old enough.

They were a devoted couple, and both of them reveled in the nursery business, where Beulah had always worked beside Felix with the same gusto he had for all the growing things. Together they had raised four strapping boys, all grown now, and whom they had hoped would one day join them in the family business. But this was not to be. They had all made their way in other professions. This turn of events disappointed the Dalgrens but made them no less proud of their successful sons, who came home often for visits.

Beulah, a stout but pretty-faced woman, was potting plants at the back of the greenhouse and waved an enthusiastic welcome to Mrs. Manning as the group entered. Felix shouted for Beulah to join them and introduced her to Jeb. She was as warm and sincere as her husband and showed her pleasure at meeting Jeb, telling him she was happy that she was helping that sweet Mrs. Manning. Then the serious business of careful selection began.

It took almost an hour of deliberation, but they finally chose six plants, with the aid of much advice and instruction from both the Dalgrens. The colors were pronounced magnificent by Mrs. Manning; deep pink (almost magenta), bright pink, and white with a pale, pink fringe on the petals.

Both Felix and Beulah helped Jeb carry their selections to the car, and waved them a happy farewell.

Jeb was grateful that the ride back was uneventful. Mrs. Manning drove at a snail's pace. Probably didn't want to upset her new "pets" in the trunk of the car.

Chapter Fifteen

Jeb had set in the Azaleas with Mrs. Manning hovering over him like a nervous mother, and Daisy, who was outside again, playing in the emptied pots. He carefully worked acid crystals into the alkaline soil along with some peat to keep the soil beneath the new plants from packing hard, and, of course, added some of their special "magic elixir".

Jeb had read that sometimes flowering shrubs were quite temperamental about being uprooted and moved. This year, blooms might be pretty sparse until the plants got settled comfortably in their new location. The two of them knew not to expect too much until next year. For now, all they could do was wait, watch, and water.

Billy and Hack still came once a week. In fact, Hack seemed to have shaped up his act and at least tried to be more respectful; or at best to say nothing sassy. He had been on, what was for Hack, his best behavior. The other two boys had talked about it and giggled behind his back, wondering if something was wrong with this "new" Hack. One day he was so syrupy sweet polite to Mrs. Manning, Jeb and Billy thought they might get sick. But she seemed to like this Hack a whole lot better, so they let it drop. But when Mrs. Manning would go into the house, Hack would mumble something about intensely disliking the "old lady's" lecture on agriculture. Billy and Jeb only shook their heads when he turned back into the "old" Hack.

Hack and Billy worked mostly on the lawn. Mrs. Manning's nurseryman, Felix, had delivered bags and bags of grass seed, mixed types of fescue, long and short leaf, blue grass and rye.

The lawn encompassed most of the entire hillside and also grew around the drive in front of the house and a good portion of the side yards. Under Mrs. Manning's tutelage, the boys worked diligently, seeding and spreading fertilizer and pesticides to cut down on weeds and the pesky lawn grubs and insects.

Sometimes they raked after they mowed. She said this gave the roots some air and allowed the grass to breathe, spread, and grow stronger. Naturally, these grass clippings went on the "stink pile" to start the process over again for next year. Sometimes they just left the clippings lay on the grass. Mrs. Manning said this would act as a moist blanket when they watered for the weeks when there wasn't enough rain.

Jeb watched the boys' progress every step of the way and learned as they did. Every chance he had when he finished early, he would give Billy and Hack a hand because the lawn work was a mighty chore as well as the gardens. His job had been to replant the bedding plants they had taken out to put in the Azaleas. Now he was setting in many of the annuals.

All of them worked at a pace, including Mrs. Manning, to get the yard spruced up for the growing and blooming part of the year. Every project they finished made Mrs. Manning as happy as a lark and she was full of praise for all of them.

The vegetable garden was all set in. The lawn had been raked, reseeded, and fertilized. The flower beds were all prepared and Jeb had put in the new annual bedding plants. He was proudest of his beloved Pansies, which were the first ones set in and going like gang-busters.

Jeb had the devil of a time with Daisy, who thought any newly-dug ground was fair territory for her to play in or potty in. He felt as if he spent half his time shooing her away. This kind of treatment didn't sit too well with Daisy, who refused to sit on his lap for the better part of a week. She was, of course, punishing him for neglecting and chastising her.

As spring turned to summer, weeding began in earnest. Lord, Jeb thought, where did they come from over and over again, literally springing up overnight. Whatever you did, nothing seemed to discourage them. Maybe someday he'd have a WEED garden. It sure would make things a whole lot easier.

Billy was a big help with weeds because his folks had a garden and he knew enough about what to pull and what not to. Hack would do most anything but the weeds. He simply detested the job and considered it beneath him. Jeb thought it was better that way because the one time he had worked with him trying to get rid of some weeds, Hack had pulled up most of the things Jeb had just planted.

Most times Jeb was plumb tuckered out when the work was finished for the day. When he was there alone, he knew he could look forward to having a cool drink and sitting for a spell before he left for home. He had put away the tools in the garage and was heading for the porch when he heard voices. As he rounded the corner of the house, he was amazed to see Mrs. Manning sitting on the porch talking to George Raven's Wing.

Jeb was so surprised, he couldn't move. Mrs. Manning spotted him and beckoned him to come up to join them. Slowly, he moved toward the pair and sat on the top step with his back against the post. She had set a tray with a plate of cookies, a pitcher, and two glasses on the porch table.

Jeb looked around for Daisy, who was nowhere to be seen. Pretty soon, though, he spied the tip of a furry, yellow tail sticking out from beneath a large rose bush beside the porch. He smiled, thinking the cat had better sense than he did staying away from anyone connected with the ghost.

"Would you like something to drink, George?"

He nodded, "Water, please, Amanda."

"Just a minute. I'll get it for you." She went back into the house.

Uncomfortable, left alone with the old man, Jeb stared silently at his hands. The Crow looked him over and then gazed around the yard. "Amanda's garden is good," said the deep voice. "You do this work?"

The vibrant timbre of the voice startled Jeb, but he looked up and replied. "Yessuh. Well, uh, some of it...the flowers, mostly, I guess."

"Amanda is happy?" George queried.

"I reckon so. I hope so. I like the work," Jeb said diffidently.

"It is right that a man likes the work he does," said Raven's Wing, nodding his head in affirmation.

Mrs. Manning came out on the porch again and handed George a glass of water. Jeb stared at him in wonder that George had referred to him as a man. In his heart this pleased him greatly and eased the nervousness he felt about the old Indian quite a bit.

George drank deeply. "Your garden reflects you soul, Amanda, child."

Mrs. Manning raised her eyebrows quizzically. "My goodness, but I think you do flatter me, George. All I know is that beauty makes my heart glad." She poured juice for Jeb and herself.

"This, I can see," he said, smiling as he studied her.

The three of them were companionably quiet for a moment. George drank again and rising, placed his glass on the table. Looking all about him, he stretched and put a hand to rub the lower part of his back. "Thank you, Amanda," he said. Then he looked directly at Jeb. "The work is good, Jebediah. You have done well." With that he walked down the porch steps and strode to the street.

Jeb looked after George's retreating back. *He remembered my name*, he silently marveled. Jeb was extremely pleased for reasons he didn't even understand. Daisy dashed up the steps and jumped into his lap.

"I think George is finally beginning to show his age, just as I do," Mrs. Manning stated sadly. "I do hope his grandfather is freed before he is."

Chapter Sixteen

"Miz Manning, how come you don't have any grandchildren?" Jeb asked innocently. He had heard his mother talking about the pity of it that Mister Carter had never had any children and what a wonderful grandmother Miz Manning would have been.

The devastated look on Mrs. Manning's face told him he'd overstepped himself again, a long way this time.

"I'm sorry, Miz Manning. It was right forward and too personal for me to ask you that. I'm real sorry. Please excuse me," Jeb said pleadingly.

A minute passed before she said anything and Jeb hung his head regretfully.

"No...no. It's quite all right, Jebediah. It's only natural that you should be curious that a woman as old as I should have no grandchildren," she paused, looking very sad. "To tell you the truth, that fact is one of the greatest disappointments of my life. But it simply was not to be." She hesitated again.

They were resting on the rocks above the lawn under the huge, old Sycamore. Daisy was hunkered down between them, staring at the sun dial and twitching her tail back and forth nervously.

"Did you know that Carter had once been married?"

"No, Ma'am. I didn't know that," Jeb said quietly.

"He was married eight years to a wonderful woman named Sandra. Sandra Louise Davidson, before their marriage. He met her at the University, just as I had met his father there. They were very happy, very well suited, I would say. My husband and I both adored her. We were so delighted for Carter," she stopped talking for a moment, absorbed in thinking about the past. Then she continued slowly.

"Sandra and he wanted children very much and were quite disheartened when this didn't happen right away. They consulted doctors and went to clinics. No one could discover an actual plausible physical reason for their childlessness." A look of pure grief came over Mrs. Manning's face.

"Our beloved Sandra was diagnosed with cancer at the age of twenty-nine. It was rapid and deadly. The pity was, they could do nothing for her, not even to prolong her life. Thankfully she didn't have long to suffer. She was gone within six months. It was a devastating thing for us to see the life just ebb out of her."

"Oh, Miz Manning, I'm so sorry I brought this up. I didn't mean for it to hurt you so much," Jeb murmured, gently touching her arm. She took his comforting hand and squeezed it.

"It's occasionally good to remember someone you dearly loved, Jebediah. To celebrate in remembering the good years you had with them and be grateful for that time. My husband and I were so aggrieved by the loss, but Carter was undone completely. We worried so much about him, his father and I. Then, when Carter's father died, he seemed to put it behind him, become stronger. Mainly for my sake, I think, and because immersing himself in work at the paper helped him cope with his grief and despair for the loss of both his wife and his father."

"How long ago did this happen, Miz Manning?" Jeb asked softly.

"We buried Sandra ten years ago, and my husband passed away three years later. Both Carter and I are wounded hearts for losing two people we loved so dearly." She took a deep breath and stretched her neck, trying to relieve some of the tension. "But you see, my husband and I were granted fifty-two long, happy years together. Carter and Sandra are the ones who were cheated somehow."

Jeb could tell this thought distressed her greatly.

"Oh, Carter regained a somewhat normal life," Mrs. Manning spoke again after a few seconds pause. "He has escorted several very nice young women to concerts and the theater and such; but no one has held his interest for long. No lasting relationship ever resulted. Carter still seems so lonely...so terribly alone."

The cat stepped onto her legs and rubbed her head against Mrs. Manning's chest. Mrs. Manning hugged Daisy's furry body close to her breast as if deriving some little comfort from her warm, four-footed friend.

Jeb was disconsolate for bringing up the subject. "I am really so very sorry, Miz Manning, for bringing up something that has caused you to be so sad."

"What's past is past, Jebediah. No matter how difficult it is to talk about loved ones who are gone, sometimes it acts like a catharsis for the mind to do just that. I think, perhaps, inadvertently you have given me an idea and set me on the positive path of a worthy project."

Jeb looked at her, surprised, with a question in his eyes.

"I have traveled all over the world in my time, Jebediah. I made lasting friends wherever I went, many with whom I still correspond," Mrs. Manning seemed less downhearted.

"My formal writing, years ago, was recognized even nationally, and I also made friends and acquaintances in the professional area of the Press. I realize, now, that all that writing of letters has become somewhat of a burden to me. I think I feel the need for a corresponding secretary coming on." She stood up and set Daisy on the ground. A crafty, calculating look came to her face and her eyes began to sparkle brightly.

Jeb was amazed at the abrupt change of subject and was utterly confused by her suddenly smiling attitude.

"Come on, let's get back to work."

She walked briskly to the nearest flower bed, knelt and began pulling off dead blossoms and poking around distractedly. Almost overcome with curiosity at her suddenly altered attitude, Jeb followed and began to work beside her. But Mrs. Manning seemed preoccupied and unable to concentrate on the task.

Presently, she stood up and said, "Please, go ahead with what you are doing, Jebediah. I must go into the house. There are some very important phone calls I need to make." And then she was off, walking with a light step Jeb hadn't seen for quite a while. He shook his head in complete bafflement.

Women! Young or old, you just can't figure 'em! He finished the weeding and left for home.

That night it was Jeb's turn to clear the table after supper and help his mother put the kitchen to rights. She was loading the dishwasher, when Jeb decided he better have a talk with her, since they were by themselves.

"Momma," he began, "Something right peculiar is going on with Miz Manning. She was acting kind of strange today." He told her about the awkward question he had asked her and how badly he had felt about it afterwards. He related all Miz Manning had told him about Mister Carter and his wife and her dying and all, how sad she had been, almost to the point of tears. He said he just couldn't understand it when all of a sudden she snapped out of her doldrums and started talking about hiring a secretary to write letters for her. It had him in a quandary as to what had changed her so quick.

Laticia listened attentively for a little while, and seemed lost in her own thoughts. "Jeb," she said thoughtfully, looking him straight in the eye, "I don't know exactly what that all means, but I have in mind that Miz Manning is about to try a little matchmaking, maybe. Now, I'm not sure, but from what you've told me, that's my best guess. But, you listen to me now, and no matter what comes around, you keep still about this, 'cause I may be wrong. You hear me?"

Jeb nodded in compliance with her wishes. As he walked upstairs to his room, he was still pondering the unfathomable workings of women's minds. None of it made any sense to him. He thought maybe his Momma might be about as tetched in the head as Miz Manning.

 *Chapter Seventeen*

Jeb and his family went to the movies together one night, all six of them. They saw a film called "Ghost". It was about a man who had been killed and didn't realize at first that he was dead. When he finally knew that no one could see him, he set about trying to communicate with the living world in order to find out who had murdered him so he could be avenged.

Everybody enjoyed the movie and especially liked the role of the flaky seance lady, played by a versatile actress who would later receive an Academy Award as best supporting actress for her portrayal.

They were riding home in the car and talking about the show; the scenes each had liked best, what scenes had been scary, the things they all thought were so funny, and some parts that were sad enough they made you cry, or want to. They laughed and chatted and enthused and rehashed, enjoying the whole evening all over again.

Naomi had hidden her face in Laticia's lap during a few scenes that scared her. Eli was being tough and macho, big time, because his father had let him drive the car tonight. He boasted that he thought the whole thing was pretty silly and he hadn't been scared one little bit. Nobody said anything about the fact that this particular movie brought to mind the ghost in Miz Manning's cistern. That was too touchy a subject to even mention.

Riding in the back seat with Naomi and Momma, Jeb's thoughts were making exactly that connection.

The weather had been very hot for an entire week, but the morning today had brought some badly needed rain, a virtual downpour. Naturally, the afternoon had been hot and steamy, extremely humid and uncomfortable. As evening came on, a cool front moved into the area and brought welcome relief. There was a bright, full moon, but some fog appeared in spots where the cooler air drifted across the hot, wet earth.

Jeb noticed they were on the street which ran in front of Miz

Manning's property. They would shortly be coming to the drive directly opposite the cistern where he always walked up the hill to work. Jeb thought about closing his eyes and just riding on by. But he couldn't help himself, he simply had to look.

The yard was there, all right, almost as plain as day, shadowed by the huge trees, the sun dial in the center of the lawn, brightened by the moonlight. Before his very eyes, a pale mist rose around the cistern, wavering, shimmering, and spiraling slowly upwards. Jeb's eyes grew enormous and seemed glued to the spot. Was the foggy mist taking the shape of a man? Was his mind playing tricks on him? Shivers prickled his neck and ran down his spine, his skin broke out in goose flesh.

Then they were past the spot and on their way home. Jeb's breath came in short little gasps. The rest of his family were still talking idly. They hadn't seemed to notice anything peculiar. Maybe it was only his imagination. Lord, he hoped it had just been his imagination.

Jeb leaned his head against the back of the seat, squeezed his eyes tightly shut and silently concentrated. *I didn't see anything! I didn't see ANYTHING! I DIDN'T SEE ANYTHING!*

Soon they were at home. Jeb was the first one in bed.

Chapter Eighteen

The next day, Jeb was having a hard time even thinking about going to work at Mrs. Manning's. When he finally got there he thought everything looked to be as normal as peach pie. Ha!

On the porch, Mrs. Manning was talking to a most attractive woman. Jeb thought she might be pretty old, maybe forty or so.

"Oh, Jebediah, I'm glad you're here. Please come up. I want you to meet Mrs. Lockyer." She turned to the woman. "Evelyn, this is Jebediah Jenkins. He's my right arm around here, and getting to know the gardens almost as well as I do. I'm very proud of all the work he has done in the yard."

Jeb was enormously pleased by her praise and greeted the woman shyly. "Hello, Miz Lockyer. Nice to meet you." She offered him her hand and he shook it gently. "Nice to meet you, too, Jebediah," she said pleasantly.

"Just Jeb, Ma'am," he said quietly...hopefully.

"And you may call me Evelyn," she smiled.

Jeb didn't think his folks believed it would be right and polite to call someone that old by their first name but he didn't want to offend her. "Maybe it's better if I call you MISS Evelyn."

"Done!" she laughed. "Miss Evelyn it is!"

Mrs. Manning laughed, too, as if he were her prized pupil. Daisy, who had been sniffing warily at Mrs. Lockyer's shoes, began winding in and out between her feet and rubbing against her legs. Jeb thought evidently Miss Evelyn had met muster and now had the "cat-manager's" stamp of approval.

"Evelyn works at the Post Office and has agreed to be my part-time, corresponding secretary in her spare hours," Mrs. Manning smiled sweetly, like a feline lapping at a bowl of cream. "She has a son about your age in school here. Maybe you know him. Thad Lockyer?"

"Yessum," Jeb replied, "I know Thad. We have a gym class together." Daisy, finished with her initial approval greeting, began to coax Jeb for some attention. He picked her up and stroked her ears.

Evelyn Lockyer had lived in Topeka, Kansas most of her life. She had married Matthew Lockyer as soon as she graduated from high school. They were completely content with their lives and their two children, Thaddeus and Jennifer, a girl born three years after their son. Matthew had been a teacher in the Kansas school system. He taught in several small towns and came to the Valleyville High School to teach history five years ago, a step up the teaching ladder for him. The family lived in what had been an old farm house, which they had renovated, on the edge of Valleyville where the town had grown out to meet it.

Two years after they settled there, Matthew was driving to school early one winter morning. The roads had been slick and icy. There was a collision of several cars, sliding out of control on the highway leading into town. He had been killed instantly. Evelyn was completely devastated when it happened. For a while, the children seemed lost in an endless depression.

But she was a survivor. A pretty, outgoing woman who genuinely liked people and had a healthy zeal for life. With the help of her Valleyville friends and neighbors, she had rallied and eventually managed quite well in spite of her loneliness. The children also had recovered with their mother's staunch love and support, and by her example. Finally, they, too, were acting like normal young kids once again.

Evelyn successfully took the Civil Service examination and went to work in the Postal System. She and Mrs. Manning shared, in common, a great love of flowers. They had met at the local Garden Club meetings. Evelyn liked Mrs. Manning and was pleased and grateful when she had been given the opportunity for a minimum of a few hours extra work. She really admired the wit and vitality of the spunky, little Mandy Lil Manning, who seemed to know everything about the plants and flowers they both took such delight in.

The ladies excused themselves and went into the house to begin the serious business of correspondence. Jeb set Daisy down on the porch step and went to the vegetable garden to set the sprinklers.

It had been so hot for a time the tomatoes were looking mighty puny. In spite of the deluge of rain yesterday morning, it had come so quickly most of it had run off. Down deep, the soil was still dry as a bone.

He stopped, holding the hose in mid-air. Suddenly it struck him like a hammer on an anvil. This was what Momma had meant about matchmaking. Miz Manning didn't really need any letter writing help. She had picked Miss Evelyn out for Mister Carter!

Lord, try to figure women! Poor Mister Carter won't even know what hit him. He'll never realize he's walking like the unsuspecting fly into the spider's web.

Jeb started to snicker. It developed into a chuckle as he started the watering, then into outright laughter. He was so tickled he just couldn't stop. Mrs. Manning stuck her head out the porch door, inquiring what all the fun was about.

Lord, forgive me! I'm going to lie. Well, just a small white lie for the good of the cause and to cover my butt for having so much fun when I ought to be seriously working.

"I'm only watching some of Daisy's antics, Miz Manning. Sometimes she can act real silly," he was still chuckling heartily.

Mrs. Manning stared at Daisy lazing sleepily on the edge of the porch. "Oh," she said puzzled, and disappeared into the house.

Almost got caught that time, Jeb thought, relieved. *Better keep my nose to the grindstone like Pop says; wait a while and watch the rest of this show Miz Manning's got planned out.* He began to apply himself to the tasks he had set out to do.

Jeb was not in the least surprised to see Mister Carter's car come up the drive along about five o'clock. He shook his head and grinned, waving to him as Carter rounded the drive next to the house.

There goes the innocent lamb about to be made into lamb chops, mused Jeb gleefully to himself.

As Jeb was coiling up the hoses against the side of the house at the vegetable garden, Gaddy Taylor came out onto the porch carrying a huge tray with pitchers and glasses, and a plate of little cakes. "Jeb, Miz Manning say for you to come over when you're finished and have a drink." She sounded muffed as usual. "She say she want you to tell Mister Carter all about your important work in the yard." With this information bluntly imparted, she flounced back into the house.

He had thought today there wouldn't be any refreshments because they would be too busy with the corresponding; or else Miz Manning would want to have their own tea party alone for the start of her matchmaking. The three of them came out to the porch just as he was taking a sack of weeds back to the trash can beside the garage.

"Jeb!" Carter hailed him. "Great job! The yard looks beautiful." Jeb walked reticently to the porch steps. He was pretty spooked about horning in on what he thought was Mrs. Manning's game plan.

"Yessuh, thank you, Mister Carter. I think it looks right nice, myself. Your Momma's taught me a whole lot," he smiled, ducking his head.

Mrs. Manning offered him a small cake and a glass of lemonade. She asked him to tell Carter about all the work being done on the yard this week. This confused Jeb a bit since it was the usual stuff they did every week, but he wanted to oblige her. He was trying to think of what to say when Gaddy pushed the porch door open forcefully and butted in.

"I'm 'bout done Miz Manning," she stated, looking pointedly at Jeb as if he was an upstart who didn't know his place. "Lest you want me to stay for something else?" she added wistfully.

"No. No, Gaddy. This is fine. Thank you very much and I'll see you next week," she dismissed her cordially.

Gaddy swooshed out in her inimitable way, leaving a characteristic "humph" in her wake.

Evelyn Lockyer looked perplexed; but Carter and Mrs. Manning were so used to Gaddy's ways they didn't appear to notice.

Jeb knew she was jealous because he was getting to stay with them and she wasn't. She felt slighted. He knew he'd probably get the brunt of it the next time he saw her.

Jeb was trying to explain about some of the things being done in the yard; but he noticed how Mister Carter's eyes kept straying to take a look now and then at Miss Evelyn. He couldn't fault Mister Carter, though. Miss Evelyn was a mighty fine looking lady, even for being middle aged. She had dark blond hair that fell on her shoulders like poured honey, eyes as blue as Morning Glories and a smile that was for real.

He wondered if Miss Evelyn had any idea what Mrs. Manning was up to, or if she was an innocent "lamb", too. Lord, he hoped Miz Manning knew what she was doing. Hoped she wasn't going to get caught for meddling.

Presently, he excused himself and went home. He couldn't wait to give his Momma a progress report. She was smart as a whip and so right.

Jeb also wondered offhandedly if Mrs. Manning was planning to say anything to Miss Evelyn about the ghost in the cistern. Probably not.

# *Chapter Nineteen*

It was mid-summer and Jeb was trying to keep some contact with Cordelia. Because there were no school classes or games, he was hard put to see her at all. He was pondering over this predicament one afternoon as they again dug up some bulbs which had doubled too quickly.

They had been digging around all the trees and were now working pretty close to the cistern; but Jeb was preoccupied with his thoughts and didn't pay much attention. Daisy was crouched down under the Cedars with her tail twitching a mile a minute.

As he stared at the bushy trees above Daisy, Jeb questioned Mrs. Manning.

"Miz Manning, I been meaning to ask you what those ugly, rusty blobs are hanging off all the Cedars? Looks like somebody pelted them with a bunch of juicy, rotten oranges."

She glanced over at the small group of trees across from them, studying the little grove of Cedars interestedly.

"Those splotches are Cedar Apple Rust, Jebediah. It is a two-host organism. Doesn't seem to bother the Cedar trees very much except to be deposited there by certain moths and cause those hideous patches for a time. The damage comes later when the spore dries and infects the apple trees, insinuating a terrible rust to the trees and the fruit," she stated mater-of-factly. "They really are truly an abomination to the eye. It looks as if some ghoul left over from Halloween tried to decorate for Christmas...and failed miserably."

Jeb laughed, shaking his head. Miz Manning sure could paint some funny pictures with her strange ideas. Even so, he learned a lot.

The wheelbarrow was half full of the labeled sacks of bulbs, and they were resting before the trek up to the garage.

"Miz Manning, can I ask you something kind of personal?"

Mrs. Manning leveled herself up and sat on the edge of the sun dial. "Ask away, Jebediah. And I'll reserve my answer until I hear the question."

Jeb still got the heebie jeebies thinking about that cistern and he didn't think he could get up the courage to actually sit on it. So he sat on the grass cross-legged in front of her. "I want to know if you know something about girls." He was timidly looking at the ground.

Oh, my! she thought, gazing up at the sky. *It has been a long time since I've had this conversation. I wonder if I'm up to it. Maybe I'm entirely too old*, she mused, rubbing her temples.

"Just what is it you wish to know, Jebediah?" she replied, guardedly.

"Well, you see, there is this girl I met in school. Her name's Cordelia. She's real pretty and real popular with everybody, even the teachers. She's awful nice and I like her a lot," Jeb paused, taking a deep breath. "I haven't seen much of her this summer, and I don't even know if she likes me at all..." Jeb ran out of words to explain further.

Mrs. Manning nodded, looking appropriately serious, but inwardly relieved. "I see. Well, that is a special problem for young folks your age. You are not yet an adult and no longer a child. You have all the size and hormones of a grown person but are not quite sure of this new human being who is evolving from your mind and body."

Lord, she's gonna give it to me about the birds and bees, Jeb thought, and flinched at the notion.

"During this physical and mental revolution..." Mrs. Manning continued much to Jeb's dismay.

Whatever made me think I could put such a question to Miz Manning of all people? Because I trust her, I guess. There's no way out now. By the look on her face, she's into it.

"Adolescents are literally on the cusp," Mrs. Manning went on, "in a virtual transitional limbo, if there is such a thing. You are no longer children and not quite full grown. It's hard to be sure of oneself when you haven't yet gained the experience and the knowledge you need to deal easily with other people, especially the opposite gender. Oh, girls know all about girls because that's what they are; and it's the same for boys. But it's difficult to know how to act and react to the opposite sex when neither of you is familiar with what kind of person the other is yet."

Jeb was inwardly cringing at what might be coming next.

"The experience of discovery is exhilarating, however, and it's what makes the world go round." She smiled encouragingly at him. "Take my sincere word for it, Jebediah. You are a very fine young man. You can be justly proud of who you are right now, and any young woman should think herself lucky to have your interest in her. It's not unusual for anyone to be a little uncertain when they're trying out their wings for the first time."

By now Jeb was looking straight at her and listening carefully.

"My advice to you is to always be yourself...always be the person you are inside yourself and you can never go wrong. Call up this girl, Cordelia. She sounds like a very nice person from your description of her. Ask her out, maybe to the movies or to have a pizza with you and just talk. I think you'll be surprised how pleased she'll be, and I'm sure everything will work out better than you expected."

Mrs. Manning stood up and stretched. Jeb was quiet as he pushed the wheelbarrow up the hill.

"Watch Carter and Evelyn sometime, Jebediah. They are older than you are, and both have been married before; but they are starting a new friendship, and it's touching to see them together. You might learn something about technique." Her eyes danced and twinkled at him.

Her little joke took some of the tension out of him and he chuckled. "Yessum, " he said, ducking his head and grinning shyly, "I'll do that."

Mrs. Manning went into the house after they walked up the hill. Jeb mulled over all the things she had said to him as he put the packaged bulbs on the shelf in the garage. He had no notion what good everything she told him was going to do for him or how it would help him in his present situation.

Today was one of the days Miss Evelyn was due to come over. Jeb knew Mister Carter probably wouldn't be far behind. Lord knows when that poor lady ever got much letter writing done, if she had any time to do it at all.

Jeb thought about the times he had seen the two of them together. They seemed to be most easy with one another, conversation flowing right natural. That was one of the things that came hard to him, striking up a casual conversation. He always felt so up tight and tongue-tied, especially around girls. He simply didn't know how to go at it without sounding like an idiot.

Like Miz Manning said, he'd have to sneak looks at them every chance he got and try to learn something.

Right on schedule, Miss Evelyn drove up to the house and waved at him. He was putting the wheelbarrow away and getting the garage straightened up. He went around the house to coil up the hoses and wash the dirt off his hands. This afternoon, after handling all those dirty bulbs, they were pretty grubby.

Sure enough, Mister Carter wasn't fifteen minutes behind. He waved, too, and went inside. Privately, Jeb thought the two of them were acting a bit like teenagers. Couldn't seem to be around each other near enough and smiling funny all the time. He couldn't believe they both hadn't a clue that Miz Manning had arranged throwing them together like this. He was still grinning about the situation, still baffled, when they all came out on the porch and invited him to join them for a drink.

Jeb was messing with Daisy, teasing her with a long piece of grass she was batting at and pouncing on. He was using the cat as a decoy so they wouldn't guess he was sneaking looks and studying them as much as he could without being caught at it.

One of Jeb's earlier questions was answered when he looked up at Miss Evelyn's face. Her eyes suddenly became enormous and her mouth was hanging open as if to catch flies. She was staring fixedly down the hill. Then he heard the nasal sing-song of the now familiar chanting.

"Well, George is back again." Mrs. Manning sounded unsurprised. Carter finally looked at Evelyn and laughed at her stunned expression. "Not to worry, Evelyn," he said, grinning as he put an arm around her shoulders. "That's only George. He's an old friend."

"He probably won't come up today. Too many people," Mrs. Manning predicted. George finished his ritual plea, turned, and saluted them on the porch, then made long strides away down the drive.

Jeb laughed as he looked again at Miss Evelyn. She was definitely in shock. He knew the feeling.

"I best be taking my leave now. Thank you for everything, Miz Manning," he said pointedly, looking straight at her. "Looks like you got a lot of explaining to do for poor Miss Evelyn."

Chapter Twenty

Later in the summer, Mrs. Manning taught him to deadhead. He thought at first they were out to kill something. But she laughed and said, "No, just the opposite." She instructed him how to pinch all the dead blossoms off the plants so other buds would set on and the plants wouldn't get so rangy or go to seed and quit blooming.

It seemed to Jeb most of these growing things had personalities of their own, just like people. They sure could get ornery if you didn't treat them the way they had a mind you ought to.

It had taken Jeb two weeks to think over all the advice Mrs. Manning had given him that one afternoon. He still concluded that girls were a very complicated subject. Even so, he had finally found enough courage to call Cordelia and ask her out for a pizza and go to a show. It had taken every ounce of gumption he could manage to make that phone call, and his hands had been sweating like they had faucets implanted in them.

Mrs. Manning had hit it right on the head again. Cordelia said she was very pleased that he had called her. She vowed she had missed seeing him at all since school let out. They went out and had a pretty good time. They had laughed a lot and enjoyed the movie, but Jeb had been so nervous he couldn't remember anything they talked about. Most of the time it seemed Cordelia did all the talking. He still couldn't make his mouth or his mind work straight when he was around girls, especially Cordelia. But Jeb was happy he had given it a try. Maybe they could do it again sometime soon if he could get his nerve up. Might be the next time would be easier. Lord, he hoped so.

The weather had been hot and dry for a long time. Jeb was having a devil of a time with the vegetable garden, especially the tomatoes. The rain, when it did come, was hard and fast and seemed to run right off the ground, just like the old days Mrs. Manning talked about when people needed all those cisterns to store water.

Naturally, he turned the sprinkler on the vegetables every day or so; but the ground was so caked and hard, it didn't seem to soak deep down to the roots like was needed to do the most good.

The tomatoes were looking droopy and sickly again, and Jeb had been struggling with the problem of what to do about it for quite a spell. Finally, he had taken a notion to make a mud dam around them to see if that would do the trick and hold the water longer.

He started for the garage to get the things he needed when Miss Evelyn drove up the hill and waved at him.

"Hi, Jeb. Good to see you. Isn't it a beautiful day?"

Jeb figured she must have taken the news of Mister Raven's Wing and the haunted cistern in stride. "Good to see you, too, Miss Evelyn," he smiled. "It sure is nice today. Mighty fine!" Jeb went into the garage as Evelyn got out of her car and entered the house.

He dragged out an old galvanized tub and set it on the metal table near the house under the peach tree. He put in plain dirt, added peat and some of the "magic" stuff from last year's finished compost heap. Then he turned on the hose and added water. He stuck his hands in and started the task of mixing it thoroughly.

Gaddy Taylor came out to sweep the porch and was eyeing him curiously. "What in the world is that awful mess you making, Jeb Jenkins?" She placed her hands on her hips in her bossiest attitude. "If I don't miss my guess, your work 'round here don't include making mud pies," she stated, shaking an authoritative finger at him.

Her fussing and fretting was a nearly every week occurrence with Jeb; and he took it with a mental shrug.

"Now, no need for you to take on so, Miz Taylor. I'm experimenting with something I hope will do some good for the tomatoes."

"I don't know what good that yucky stuff gonna do 'em, lessen you gonna make 'em up in black face to look more like you!" She jeered sassily at him. "I'm gonna tell Miz Manning you out here fooling around, wasting time she's paying you for." With that exit line, Gaddy stormed back into the house talking a blue streak to herself.

Jeb sighed deeply. "Lord, deliver us from that know-it-all woman," he breathed in frustration.

His concoction was getting too thick to work with. It needed more water. What Jeb had in mind was making a makeshift dam around each tomato plant to hold as much water for as long as possible. First, he intended to take a trowel and loosen the soil around the plant so it could absorb more moisture. He wasn't sure it would work, but he figured it wouldn't hurt to give it a shot. Lord, he'd added too much water. It looked like mud soup.

He decided to give it a chance to soak up and air out a little before he began. He had other work he could do while he waited. Jeb was rolling the hose up when Mrs. Manning strolled nonchalantly out of the house toward the tub under the tree. She was wearing a white blouse and white slacks. Like a flash, Gaddy was back swishing her broom as fast as Daisy could swish her tail when she was annoyed.

"Old witch!" Jeb's mind pictured Gaddy with her broom, but he squelched the thought quickly.

A puzzled Mrs. Manning circled the table with the tub. Miss Evelyn stepped onto the porch to see what had gotten Mrs. Taylor's dander up. She, too, peered curiously at the muddy goo.

"What have we here?" Mrs. Manning asked in wonder. "It looks very interesting," she stated cautiously, remembering her vow to trust Jebediah, no matter what.

"That's something I'm trying out to see if it will help the failing tomatoes, Miz Manning. Don't you get too close. That stuff's real messy and I don't want you to get all dirty, now, you hear," he warned nicely.

"But what exactly is it, Jebediah?" she asked, leaning down very near to sniff at it, not heeding his words. At that moment, the last diehard, shriveled peach gave up the ghost and plopped into the mud beside Mrs. Manning's face.

There was a moment of stunned silence. Nobody dared breathe. Then Jeb was running to her and as she raised her head, he stopped on a dime. He felt his stomach rolling. Lord help him, he didn't want to laugh. He tried valiantly not to, but the sight of Mrs. Manning with a black face simply undid him. The chuckles started to erupt out of him. He was helpless to stop them.

She took her fists and cleared the goop away from her eyes and looked over at him. That sight sent him into gales of uncontrollable laughter. He had to lean against the peach tree for support. When he could get a breath, he squealed, "Oh, Miz Manning, I'm sorry for laughing," he gasped out, "but you look just like me with blue eyes!" Then he was off again, roaring and clutching his sides.

Gaddy stormed out in the yard like an enraged mother tiger. "Jebediah Jenkins, you ought to be ashamed of yourself. How could you do such a bad thing to Miz Manning? Say such a ugly thing? Shame on you!" She gathered a very dirty Mrs. Manning to her and headed towards the house. "Come on, Miz Manning. Gaddy will get you all cleaned up. You can take care of that boy later!" she yelled over her shoulder.

The front of Mrs. Manning's white blouse was a muddy mess and dirty water dripped from her chin and her hands onto her snowy white trousers.

On the porch, Evelyn stood with compressed lips, biting her tongue. She stepped down to take Mrs. Manning's other arm in assistance. Jeb knew he was in big trouble, but he truly could not stop laughing. He was subsiding into giggles and slid down the tree in a sitting position because his legs wouldn't hold him up.

As Gaddy opened the screened door to let them in, she couldn't resist a parting shot. "You gonna get yours, you bad boy! Shame, shame, shame on you, Jebediah Jenkins!"

Miss Evelyn was the last one to enter the house. She turned to Jeb and said, in a very stern voice, "Yes! Shame on you, Jebediah!" But she was smiling broadly and winked at him. Jeb was completely dumfounded.

Eventually, Jeb calmed down and mudded up the tomatoes the way he had planned to. If this was going to be his last day working here, he decided to finish the job he had started. He only hoped that his idea worked and he wasn't in complete disgrace. But he sorely doubted it.

He washed out the mud tub and was putting it away in the garage along with the hose when Carter drove up. At the same time, Gaddy's car shot by, barely missing them both. She took the "ski jump" in the same manner it was Mrs. Manning's habit to do, which was most unusual for Gaddy, who pampered her old wreck like it was something special.

Carter got out of his car and walked around the back of the house to the porch, motioning for Jeb to come with him. Jeb was loath to go, hating the thought of having to face Miz Manning again after he had disgraced himself laughing so hard at her. Just remembering the sight of her made him smile a little anyway. *My goodness, but she had looked mighty funny!*

He was resigned to his fate, deciding the only manly thing to do was apologize to her right before she fired him.

It was Miss Evelyn, this time, who set a tray on the porch table. She greeted both Carter and Jeb with an unusually big smile. A cleaned up Mrs. Manning followed her outside and sat down, looking somber. Jeb ducked his head to keep from looking her in the eye. Miss Evelyn poured drinks and handed them around. This time a Pepsi for Jeb. He was more than surprised at that. Still, he didn't dare look up.

"Carter," began his mother, "there was an extraordinary happening here this afternoon." She sounded so serious, Jeb could almost feel the ax beginning to fall. "Jebediah concocted a huge pot of glop." Carter looked askance at Jeb, frowning, then turned his attention to his mother questioningly.

Mrs. Manning commenced to relate the events leading up to and after the mud bath in such a straight-faced, witty way that Carter began to laugh out loud. Jeb could hardly believe his ears. He chanced a quick look at her and was awash with relief to see her eyes were twinkling. Miss Evelyn was laughing also and nodded her reassurance to him.

By the time Mrs. Manning was finishing the story, Carter and Evelyn were laughing uproariously, and Mrs. Manning was, too. Jeb was smiling guardedly; but Mrs. Manning looked straight at him and said, "You were right, Jebediah. I looked just like you with blue eyes."

That did it. They all howled together at the absurdity of it. Daisy leaped onto the porch to see what all the fuss was about, and gazed at her favorite humans as if they had lost their minds.

Lord, be praised, sighed Jeb, *I'm saved again!*

Chapter Twenty-One

One day a few weeks later when Jeb arrived to work in the yard, Carter Manning was waiting for him.

"Jeb, my mother hasn't been feeling very well lately, I'm going to take her to see the doctor this afternoon. She told me to ask you to go on about your chores. She says you know what has to be done."

Jeb's stomach lurched in a flip-flop. Lord, he didn't want something to be wrong with his friend, Miz Manning.

Carter was waiting for him the next day, also. "Mother is going to have surgery, Jeb. She won't be here for a while, so I hope you'll carry on with your work as best as you can."

The devastated look on Jeb's face must have registered his distress to Carter. "It's her gall bladder, Jeb. the doctors assure me that she'll be fine. I'll try to keep you posted on her progress."

Jeb was very depressed and worried the rest of the afternoon, but just working seemed to ease him a little. Two days later he decided to go to the hospital to see Mrs. Manning. He wanted to take her something but he thought it was foolish to take her flowers, like most people were apt to do, since she had her own yard full of them. He finally concluded that a nice card would again be the best choice.

He chose one that read, DEAR FRIEND...GET WELL SOON. At the hospital, he was told that Mrs. Manning was no longer there. She had been discharged, they said. This information startled him. *She only just got operated on, didn't she?* In his confusion, he didn't know whether to be happy or scared to death. At a loss, he decided to go on to work in the gardens.

Jeb was halfway up the hill when he spotted Mrs. Manning sitting on the porch. He was so delighted at the sight of her that he ran the rest of the way up the hill. He stood in front of her, grinning like a Cheshire cat.

"Jebediah, you're late for work. That's not like you. What's going on? Is this a case of 'when the cat's away, the mice will play'?" Daisy must have missed her, too, because she was curled up in a sleepy ball on Mrs. Manning's lap.

He was very glad to see her looking so well and didn't mind the scolding. He just kept on smiling as he held the card out to her.

"What's this, Jebediah? A peace offering?" But Jeb noticed she was smiling and her eyes were dancing.

"I went to the hospital to see you, Miz Manning. They told me you weren't there. That's why I'm late." She read the card and looked up at him.

"Well, for heaven's sakes. I think you really were worried about me, Jebediah. It was very thoughtful of you to be concerned, and I thank you for the nice card."

He would never be aware that this card also would go into the considerable stash of sentimental memorabilia, dear to her heart.

"I kind of thought after an operation and all, you'd be in the hospital for a week or so," Jeb said, still beaming.

"That's usually the way, Jebediah, but I had laparoscopic gall bladder surgery." The uncomprehending look on his face prompted her to explain. "Yes, it was new to me, too; but it is done routinely nowadays." She then lapsed into her teacher mode.

"Instead of the very large incision that's so difficult to recover from, they make three little incisions near the navel. One for a very small light, one for a tiny camera, and one for the scalpel. The camera, with the help of the light, hunts for the offending gall bladder, and when the surgeon has it in sight on a TV screen above the patient, he can go in the other incision with the knife and rid his patient of the pesky old thing. He puts in a few stitches and covers them with very small bandages. It's quite a remarkable procedure."

Jeb's eyes got wider and wider with this revelation. "In popular un-medical-like language, they refer to this as "band-aid surgery". And fortunately for the patients, recovery time is minimal. I feel fine. A little bit sore, but otherwise fine, really. In fact, I am going to drive the car tomorrow."

Jeb looked down at his feet and shook his head thinking of all the terrible possibilities that might come out of that information. Maybe worse than the surgery.

"I'm glad you're home and doing so good, Miz Manning," he grinned sheepishly, "You just holler if you need something, you hear, and I'll be pleased to oblige."

Chapter Twenty-Two

Ever since Miss Evelyn started coming to help with the corresponding a couple of days a week, Carter had taken to stopping by to see his mother on those very same days. But after the surgery, Carter came even more often, almost every day. He usually arrived late in the afternoon to check on his mother and visit for a while, sometimes maybe not more than a few minutes. They seemed to have a pretty good relationship together from what Jeb could observe; and that kind of made him glad because he and his own mother got along right well, too.

When Jeb was through working in the yard, Mrs. Manning usually always asked him to join them for a drink and a snack. The first time this had happened a while back, Jeb had been a bit wary because Mister Carter was his boss at the paper and he thought maybe they didn't want him to horn in on their time together all the time. But they were both very pleasant to him, asking him each afternoon how things were coming along in the yard. This always made him feel important, and the fact they considered and respected his opinion filled him with a great sense of pride.

He watched carefully to see how the progress was going with the matchmaking plan. He noticed Mister Carter and Miss Evelyn seemed to be right good friends and acted very comfortable in each other's company. While he thought Miss Evelyn was a fine looking woman, he couldn't blame her for being attracted to Mrs. Manning's son.

Carter Manning was no slouch in the distinguished, masculine-good-looks department, either. He was tall and had a fine large frame. He had his mother's blue eyes and dark, wavy hair. There was a little gray creeping into his sideburns, but it seemed to give him a kind of dignified look. Lord knew he had a sense of humor. Jeb had been witness to that several times. That fact helped to keep Mister Carter from seeming too fearsome. Jeb figured everything was coming along just keen, and so far the "lambs" hadn't suspected anything about Miz Manning's meddling.

As the weeks wore on into late summer, Mrs. Manning still came outside to talk with the boys and instruct them about the work to be done that day. After the surgery, though, she seldom worked along beside Jeb anymore. That "band-aid" thing seemed to have taken a little of the starch out of her. She still pulled a few weeds here and there and pinched off some dead blooms, but her old energy was sapped some.

Hack took to becoming somewhat unreliable. He'd come if he felt like it, and other times wouldn't show up at all. This really nettled Mrs. Manning and left a lot more work for the other two boys. Hack was pretty good help when he was there, but they couldn't count on him. Privately, Jeb supposed that's why Hack had never been able to hold a job for long. He was sorry he'd ever asked him to help, especially since most times he irked Mrs. Manning so.

But what was done was done and he guessed they'd have to make the best of it. What Hack needed, Jeb thought, was a major attitude adjustment. He still hoped he could work on him, real nice and carefully, if he ever got the chance.

One Saturday, Hack did show up for work, but late. Jeb suspected he'd been drinking again. He smelled a mite suspicious, and he was acting more peculiar than he usually did. Jeb knew it wasn't exactly the right time to have his say to Hack; but he wasn't sure there would be a better time, or even if Hack would show up for work again considering his undependability of late.

Jeb started off as nice as he could manage. "Hey, Man! You been leaving a lot of your work for me and Billy when you don't get here. We need you, Hack. There's more than a lot for all of us to do around here, and the pay's real good."

"Get off my back, Jeb. I don't need you bossing me around. I get enough of that crap from my old man. I do what I wanna do. So just back off, kid. You got that?" Hack fairly snarled at him.

Jeb was really taken aback by the animosity in Hack's attitude and words. "I was just trying to give you some good advice, Hack. I didn't mean to get you all riled up."

"Well, I don't need no advice from nobody. So leave me alone."

He grabbed the rake and stormed down the hill to start raking by the cistern.

Jeb took this as an act of defiance. He had told them the story of the Indian ghost in the cistern. Billy's eyes had gotten real big and he didn't go any nearer to it than he had to. Hack had just laughed at what he considered a silly old tale and bragged, "Big deal! I don't believe in no ghosts anyways."

Jeb looked after him for a minute, shook his head, and went on about what he had been doing. He simply couldn't understand Hack; and he realized no amount of talking was going to do any good. Billy worked all morning, but left in the middle of the afternoon. Hack had worked about an hour and then he was gone, too.

Later that same afternoon when his work was finished for the day, Jeb joined Carter and Mrs. Manning resting on the porch, sipping drinks. Presently, Evelyn came out to sit a spell with them, and Jeb decided to ask Mrs. Manning about how she came to live here in Kansas.

"Miz Manning, you told me once that you were born in Oklahoma. How did you come to live up here in Valleyville?"

"Well, Jebediah, I think I was about eight years old when my family moved here. About the same age as your Naomi," she smiled at him. "My father was a country doctor. When his father died, he came here to take over his father's practice. You see, back then, there wasn't another doctor around Valleyville for about thirty miles or more, so my father felt he was truly needed here. But in those days there was little money to be had. Many of my father's patients paid for his services in produce and livestock. Sometimes he would come home with a bushel of corn or potatoes. Another time it might be a couple of chickens, and sometimes even a turkey," Mrs. Manning said, shaking her head sadly. "Our family ate very well then, but for a while there was little money left over for the other things we needed. However, with the help of new friends and neighbors, we fared pretty well; and not very long after that we settled in a big, old stone house just outside of town on Freedom Hall road. The house is still there," she said reminiscently. "One of these days before too long, I may take you out there to see it."

"Yessum, I know it. We used to take rides out in the country all the time and I've seen it lots of times. I didn't know it was where you used to live, though."

"It was about the time we moved into that house that I was going through my "doctoring" stage. I must have been the bane of my father's existence. Every baby bird that tumbled from the nest, every bird with a broken wing, hen-pecked chickens, or mangy barn cats fell under my ministrations. The wonderful remedies in my father's doctor's satchel became fair game for my ailing patients. I pilfered tonics and tinctures, ointments, balms, and bandages without remorse. My parents scolded and threatened, but nothing could deter me from my 'good works'."

All three of the listeners laughed at the story, which Carter had heard many times before, but always seemed to enjoy hearing again.

"My folks never did really punish me for all that blatant misbehavior. I am still not exactly sure why they didn't, because I certainly deserved it. Oh, I got some really intense lectures on the subject. I must have finally outgrown the urge to cure."

Chuckling, Jeb blurted, "You surely must have been a little devil, way back when, Miz Manning, even worse than my little sister, Naomi." He looked up startled, realizing what he had said, just as Carter and his mother burst into gales of laughter. Evelyn looked extremely amused and smiled broadly, enjoying his gaff. Embarrassed, Jeb hung his head and thought he'd really put his foot in his mouth this time.

Finally, when he quit chuckling, Carter said, "I think you hit the nail on the head with that comment, Jeb."

His mother gave him a playful nudge in the ribs with her elbow. When Jeb understood they weren't upset with him, he began to grin guiltily.

To get them away from thinking about his bold speaking, Jeb said quietly, "Is this where you met and married your husband, Miz Manning, Mister Carter's father?"

"Oh, no you don't, Jebediah. That's another long story and you'll get me to talking on and on. We'll save that one for another day. It's getting late and your mother might scold us both for keeping you so long. Let me get my keys and run you home."

Jeb was frantically trying to think of a nice way out of that predicament when Carter spoke up and saved him.

"Never mind, Mother, I've got to get a move on. I'll be glad to drop Jeb off at his house."

Jeb nodded his thanks and waved good-bye to Mrs. Manning and Miss Evelyn. *Lord, that had been a close one!*

Chapter Twenty-Three

Later that same week, Jebediah walked around the corner of the newspaper building. He had just loaded all the trash bags in the dumpster. He was finished here for the day and was going to Mrs. Manning's house for the afternoon. As he neared the side door, she drove up in her huge car. She rolled down the window and greeted him with a smile.

"Hello, Jebediah. Lucky thing I caught you in time. I can save you the walk up to the house. Hop in."

"Oh boy, oh boy," Jeb mumbled to himself and got into the car slowly with a heavy heart. He nodded to her greeting and pasted on a smile; but she accelerated with such pressure that he was thrown back in his seat and stared in horror as the front fender missed the cement corner of the loading dock by all of two inches.

They bumped along into the alley. Luck was again on Mrs. Manning's side because the alley was clear with no cars or trucks heading their way.

Jeb let out a lung full of air in relief but sucked it back in swiftly when she drove over the curb into the street. He swallowed the lump in his throat and started praying.

Mrs. Manning was in a festive mood and chatted up a storm as she proceeded down one of Valleyville's main thoroughfares crowded with mid-day traffic. She seemed calm, cool, and unperturbed. Jeb was literally shaking in his boots. His legs felt like jelly.

"I thought it would be a treat to take a little ride," she said enthusiastically.

Some treat, Jeb thought frantically. *I hope I survive.*

Because he had a sense of impending doom, Jeb felt the need to distract himself any way he could. He glanced sideways and noticed that she was dressed to the teeth in a real nice navy blue suit with a fluffy white blouse that had lots of lace and stuff on it. And it looked like she'd had some kind of fluffing done to her hair which didn't look so matted down and stringy like it did when she had on her garden hat and was working outside. Leastways, it was nice to see her looking more like her perky old self again.

"You look mighty nice today, Miz Manning. You been out bridging with your girls...I mean the ladies?"

"No, no. Today, I've been running errands, things that pile up and won't wait any longer. I went to the bank to sign some papers and then had lunch with Carter. I thought maybe I could catch you before you started walking. Good timing, don't you think?"

Jeb shook his head. "Yes, Ma'am. Just perfect." *One more minute and I could have been outta there, gone on my own two safe feet*, he thought ruefully.

"Well, this little outing is going to be very special for me, and I hope it will at least be interesting for you."

That remark peaked Jeb's curiosity momentarily and took his mind off the traffic problem. "Where we going, Miz Manning?"

"You'll see," was all she would say with a smug smile as she turned off onto a state highway.

Lord, please, stand by! was Jeb's silent plea.

They proceeded along the highway for several miles. Thankfully there was very little traffic. Then Mrs. Manning turned again and they were headed west on a county road. For a mile or two it was paved, but the macadam ended abruptly and they bumped along on dirt and gravel with deep potholes. Mrs. Manning narrowly missed going into a deep ditch at the side of the road trying to avoid the biggest ones.

Jebediah's teeth were rattling and he held the armrest with a fierce grip. Then he spied the house ahead of them and realized where they were headed.

A very large limestone house sat far back away from the road in a grove of tall, old, Elm trees. He had been so preoccupied with their precarious trip he hadn't paid attention to the direction they were taking; but now he recognized the place from the rides he and his family had taken in the country, and knew from Mrs. Manning's description that this was her childhood home.

She must have taken a hankering to get a look at it after talking so much about it the other day, Jeb thought. He could almost feel her vibrating with excitement beside him in the car.

"Look, Jebediah. This is the house where I lived when I was a little girl. I recently discovered it has been vacant for some time and is up for sale again. I thought this might be my chance to take a good look at the old place one more time."

Though slightly rutted, the graveled driveway was in better shape than the main road had been. They rode fairly smoothly toward the house around a circular drive in front. It looked enormous to him. Jeb was impressed.

"My, my!" Mrs. Manning sighed, as she brought the car to a smooth stop. "When I was little, I always thought the house was so large; but now it seems...oh, just average size. Isn't that funny?"

Jeb thought that was very amusing since it was one of the biggest houses he had ever seen.

"It's real nice, Miz Manning, and it looks pretty big to me," he stated honestly.

They sat a moment staring at the house. For some reason, Mrs. Manning seemed reluctant to get out of the car.

Finally, she said quietly, "This house has a long and interesting history, Jebediah. It was built over a century and a half ago by a man named Mumford Hall. When the Civil War was raging, he and his wife helped many Negroes, escaped slaves or freed men running from the horror of the conflict. They would befriend them and keep them here, hidden away in the basement and barns until they could get them out to safety on the underground railroad."

"The Halls were courageous people and ahead of the times in their thinking. They took a great deal of ridicule and snubbing, and even dire threats from their friends and neighbors who suspected what they were doing. That didn't stop them, though. I imagine they saved the lives of many deserving people. That's how this old place got the name, "Freedom Hall". I have deep respect for that kind of fortitude."

Jeb was disturbed by this revelation. He could almost see the people in his mind's eye, poor, frightened and running for their lives. The thought touched him deeply and gave him a new understanding and appreciation for the life he and his family lived today.

Finally they got out of the car and looked around them. Mrs. Manning started walking across the yard toward a grove of trees. Jeb followed close behind her in case she might stumble on the uneven ground.

"See here, Jebediah. This was my father's orchard, his pride and joy. There were all kinds of fruit trees, Peach, Pear, Plum. Over there are the remnants of the grapevines. My mother used to make the most delicious jelly." Then she laughed delightedly in returning memories. "And Papa made wine in the cellar." Jeb grinned at this revelation.

"I wonder if it's still here," she said wistfully, walking farther into the grove. "Yes! Yes, there it is." Mrs. Manning hurried to a gnarled old tree and laid both hands gently on the trunk as if she were caressing a long time friend. "This is the Apple tree I used to climb almost every day. I loved this old thing. It's where I spent many a day hanging upside down." She began patting the rough trunk fondly.

That mental picture was still hard for Jeb to imagine, watching Mrs. Manning at this moment in time. The ancient tree was the worse for wear as far as he could tell. One side was in fair condition, but the other was rotted in the center and dying. The peeling bark gave it a seared and hurting look.

Mrs. Manning was quiet walking around to the back of the house, withdrawn into her own thoughts. The backyard was a jumble of weeds and discarded junk. A rusty wheelbarrow minus the wheel lay on it's side against a stump. A partly used wood pile stood haphazardly in disarray. Steel porch chairs with splotchy patches of remaining paint, unidentifiable in color, leaned askew against the house.

"Everything looks as if no one cared about it," she said sadly. Tacitly, Jeb agreed.

Farther back behind the house, an old barn leaned precariously to one side. Jeb was sure a good strong Kansas wind could do it in at any time.

"Back there," Mrs. Manning pointed to the barn, "is where I used to ride our old work horse. It was such fun. It doesn't look as if it would be fun anymore, does it?"

Jeb didn't think she was expecting an answer, more like she was talking to herself. This "treat" was turning out to be kinda disappointing for her and he felt real bad about it. But he didn't quite know what to say or how to buck her up from being so depressed.

The veranda was one of the most charming features of the old structure. It curved gracefully about the entire face of the home, adding to its stately appeal. Mrs. Manning slowly ascended the stairs and Jeb followed, watching her closely. He was fascinated by the old structure, but he knew the run-down look of the place where she had once lived as a little girl had greatly unsettled her. He could tell she was mighty upset.

They both peered in the dust-streaked windows. On the right was the living room. Jeb reckoned they must have called it the parlor way back when. As he looked inside, he thought he was looking at about the biggest room he'd ever seen. The ceilings must have been twelve or fifteen feet high. A tarnished brass chandelier hung in the center, proclaiming the grandeur of former days.

Even through the murky panes, they could see the layers of dust everywhere and cobwebs hanging from every corner. In a bayed window was an old rocking chair with broken rungs and a worn, feathered cane seat.

"When I was very young," Mrs. Manning said plaintively, "we had a big rocking chair in that same place. So pretty it was, made of hand-carved cherry wood, so often polished it glistened when the sun's rays beamed through that window, bringing a sheen to that beautiful grain. When I was tired and worn out from playing so hard, and fighting for dear life not to take a nap, even as old as I was then, my mother used to take me in her arms and sit in that chair. She would sing to me, rocking and patting until I fell asleep. It was a heavenly feeling. She was so soft and she smelled so good...like home. I miss her," old Mrs. Manning said very quietly.

Like kids looking at a toy store window, they stood a moment longer, peering in like interlopers at another day long ago. One in the faded reality of memory, the other vicariously. Abruptly, Mrs. Manning turned and started down the steps to the car. "Come along, Jebediah," she said decidedly, "I think I've had enough."

They got into the car and Mrs. Manning never looked back as

they drove away. Jeb took one last look at the decadent old mansion and tried to make sense of what had happened, what they had seen and how it had affected Mrs. Manning. He thought of all she had told him about Freedom Hall and how it redefined his thinking about his own life and the people around him.

Mrs. Manning was unusually quiet until they got back to town. Her driving was slow but not erratic. Then, suddenly she blurted, "Who was it who penned the words, 'You can't go home again?'...Well, he was right!"

Chapter Twenty-Four

The fall work began again and went well for a while. Hack hardly ever showed up anymore, so Jeb and Billy were hard pressed to get all the preparations for winter done by themselves.

Aware of his mother's recent lack of stamina and increasing frailty since her operation, Carter knew the fall work in the yard was pretty hard on just the two boys alone. Carter told Jeb to take off from the paper one extra afternoon each week and work that time at Mrs. Manning's.

Miss Evelyn mentioned that Thad couldn't help out in the afternoons because he had football practice. But she said she'd ask him if he would come on Saturdays for as long as he was needed. That sounded like good news to Jeb and Billy. They needed all the help they could get.

The weather was beautiful and Jeb relished every minute out of doors. He had the routine about down pat by now, so he could pretty well work on his own. Even though he didn't need so many instructions at present, Mrs. Manning always came out to view what he was doing and make suggestions.

He finished a little early one day and the two of them were sitting in their usual places on the porch chatting contentedly when Carter dropped by.

"The crispness in the air on this gorgeous autumn afternoon calls for hot cocoa today, Gentleman," Mrs. Manning stated. The three of them sipped with delight, and Carter said it was scrumptious and hit the spot on a cool, fall day.

It was Carter who prodded his mother into telling the story of how she had met his father.

"Oh, Carter, that's ancient history. You don't want to hear that story again," she demurred. "Sure I do, Mother, and Jeb has never heard it. Besides, he first asked you to tell us a few weeks ago. You can spin a pretty good yarn, you know."

Jeb nodded eagerly, hoping to spur her on. She took a minute to collect her thoughts and leaned back in her chair.

"Well, to go back a little way before that...my poor parents couldn't seem to get the mischief out of me; so they decided the only hope of my ever becoming a lady was to send me away to school. I spent three years in my teens at Miss Catherine Bartholamew's Finishing School for Young Ladies in Hadley, Missouri. I immediately and impudently dubbed her Catty Barthol-meow and the other girls took up the nickname behind Miss Catherine's back. You can see I was up to my old tricks again, even away from home."

Mrs. Manning told of the rules against wearing any kind of cosmetics, which were thought to "cheapen" young women. So one day, in a fit of rebellion, they painted their faces and lips with white bath powder and sketched their eyebrows on with a blood red lip rouge stealthily furnished to them by an upperclassman. She chuckled heartily remembering what a sight they had made. "I didn't get off so lightly that time, I'll tell you. I underwent a good deal of detention. My parents were duly informed and I was given a warning probation." Mrs. Manning said her folks knew at once who the instigator of that little farce had been, and several very stern letters had arrived from home posthaste.

"I don't know whether I finished that school or they finished me. I think maybe it was a draw," she nodded emphatically.

"Mother, you haven't got to the part where you met Dad yet," Carter urged kindly.

"Yes, I'm wandering, aren't I, Dear? I apologize, Jebediah, but when you've lived as long as I have you've got a lot of years to recover and are apt to get off the track now and again."

"You must have been awesome, Miz Manning. Just plain awesome," Jeb said with respect.

"Awesome, is it?" she laughed. "Well, I finally did get 'finished' enough to be present in respectable company. Anyway, after Miss Catherine's, I went off to the University of Kansas in Lawrence; and that's where I met your father, Carter. I really didn't like him at first, even though he was very popular with the other students, especially the girls," she teased. "I definitely thought he was a snob. He was two years ahead of me, you see, a 'Big Man On Campus', I think they called him, and the son of a newspaper owner and editor, while I was merely the daughter of a lowly country doctor. At the time, he never so much as looked my way. My romantic instincts didn't take hold for your father until much, much later, after I began teaching school."

Chapter Twenty-Five

J eb got home pretty late that evening, even with Mister Carter giving him a ride. But his folks didn't scold him, and his mother had saved him plenty of supper. She was used to his ways working in the yard. She also knew that he and Miz Manning chatted away after the work was done. It pleased her that Jeb and Miz Manning had such a nice relationship because she liked Miz Manning very much herself, having worked for her that time years ago. Besides, the family loved to hear all the stories of Miz Manning's young life when Jeb got home.

Jeb had chuckled to himself all the way back in Mister Carter's car, about how she and Mister Manning had become sweethearts. She said that when she finally settled down to learn something after all her school capers, she found she had quite an aptitude for foreign languages. Well, Jeb didn't think that was news. The way his Miz Manning liked to talk, it figured she'd be bound to communicate in just about any tongue.

She told how she had studied French, Spanish and Latin in school. Then said she had taken more of the same plus German and Greek at the University. *Latin AND Greek of all things*, Jeb cringed. *Ugh*, he grimaced, *worse than spinach, band-aid surgery, and that stink pile put together. That woman must be right much of a glutton for punishment*, he reasoned. But he laughed anyway, knowing all that talking stuff was pretty much right down her alley.

When he got home the family gathered round the kitchen table while Jeb ate. He told them about how she landed a job after graduation from the University of Kansas right here in the Valleyville High School teaching English, Spanish and French. Lord, what a heap of words that must have been!

One day, Mrs. Manning had told him with a far away look in her eyes, a very distinguished man came into her classroom at the school and liked to scared the daylights out of her. She said he looked so old to her, and so tall, and so pompous, and spoke in such an authoritative manner, she was really taken back a pace.

"Imperious," is what Miz Manning had called him. Jeb had looked that up in his dictionary.

The man informed her he would like to engage her for the purpose of teaching Spanish to his son. What a relief, she said, to know he wanted something so simple and so easily granted. She imagined his son to be the age of one of her students. When she realized this was the Mister Manning who owned the Valleyville newspaper, that his son was the University "Big Man", the one she thought was such a snob...well, she had nearly keeled over in a faint, she related.

Jeb's family got a big kick out of that part of the telling.

So Miss Fairchild, the teacher, began to tutor the "Big Man" once a week. As if the job weren't intimidating enough, she had agreed to go to his home where he lived with his parents, because the young couple would need to be duly chaperoned during the lessons.

Jeb's siblings thought that was a wonder because they just couldn't imagine old Miz Manning in compromising circumstances, getting carried away with a boyfriend and having to have what amounted to a referee.

The lessons started on a very business-like basis, Miz Manning had stated, until she looked deeply into Mister Manning's huge blue-gray eyes. A far away, dreamy look came onto her own eyes and Carter had to nudge her to get on with the story. "Well, that was IT for me," she had sighed. "I was lost. I could barely think how to speak English, much less Spanish. Probably the only time in my life I was speechless, more's the pity."

The lessons had lasted for three months, and, of course, the feelings were mutual. Mister Manning did learn a little Spanish, though, enough to get him by anyway; and he left immediately for South America to manage one of his father's newspapers. "Learn the ropes of the business the hard way." Miz Manning had quoted him.

Miz Manning had a difficult time with this part of the remembering. She said he was in South America for a whole year and she had pined away like a love sick Gooney Bird. She continued to teach during the time he was away. "To keep my mind off my aching heart," she had said sadly. They had written many beautiful, romantic letters to each other, she revealed. Naturally, those prized momentos were still stashed away with all the other precious souvenirs of her life.

Wistfully smiling, Miz Manning ended the story saying they were married less than a month after he returned home.

Chapter Twenty-Six

On the way to school, Jeb had to cross one of Valleyville's main intersections, Valley Street. It was so named, not only after the town, but because the roadbed lay in a kind of dip in the terrain with the land slanting up steeply on either side. It was due to this positioning that the city was ever having flash flooding there and sewer problems.

This particular fall morning, Jeb noticed that the traffic light was out and hooded. City of Valleyville trucks were parked on both sides of the street. Six city employees were digging a ditch in one of the traffic lanes close to the curb. That is to say three men were in the hole digging, and three men were standing around watching them work. They had placed orange traffic cones at the edge of the working area to alert drivers.

Jeb paused for a minute to look at the work in progress. Out of the corner of his eye, he saw a large automobile approaching the intersection at a pretty fair clip. *That resembles Miz Manning's car,* he thought idly.

As the vehicle proceeded closer without lessening speed, Jeb's eyes widened. *Oh, Lord! Stand by! It's her car.*

The workers had also seen the car and were keeping a watchful eye out. Jeb was mumbling under his breath. *Step on the brake, Miz Manning. Step on the break. Slow it down. Ma'am, slow it down, please!*

It was obvious at this point that the car was coming on and the driver did not intend to slow down. Traffic was heading to the intersection from all lanes, when the assembled group saw the directional signal begin to blink.

"Holy cow! Take cover!!" Jeb shouted to the men. By this time the workmen were very nearly paralyzed by the sight of the fast-approaching automobile. But just in the nick of time, as Mrs. Manning swerved the car around the corner, practically on two wheels, brakes screeched in all directions, shovels flew into the air and three watchers hit the ditch smack on top of the diggers. Jeb took refuge behind the large traffic pole as the orange cones sailed into the air and crashed on top of the hole full of men.

Mrs. Manning drove on unconcerned, never looking back. "Must have had something mighty potent on her mind," Jeb let out a gush of breath finally. Nothing moved for several moments. Jeb watched as the heads of the city workers came cautiously into view over the edge of the piled dirt, and peered after the car in disbelief.

Looking at the incredibly relieved faces all around him, Jeb began to chuckle in the aftermath. "Been there! Done that!" He smiled, striding confidently across the street while the traffic was still stunned and immobile.

After school, Jeb was headed for the garden, thinking about the morning's intersection incident, and wondering if Mrs. Manning had made it to and back from wherever she was going. Lord, he hoped so. She was such a nice lady, but if the truth be known, she was a real menace on the road.

Jeb was lost in his thoughts as he rounded the corner of the drive and started up the hill. The sight that greeted him was unique.

Mrs. Manning was standing on the sun dial directing a hill full of people. Cars and trucks were parked on each side of the driveway. Harry Bains and his son Daryll were unloading huge shrubs from the back of Felix Dalgren's nursery truck. Felix and Beulah were staggering across the lawn, carrying bushes, with the rooted bottoms ball-bagged in burlap. Billy, and even Miss Evelyn's son Thad, were digging holes to accommodate the new plants. Thad's practice had been cancelled so he had been pressed into service.

Mister Carter was running around with the hose to squirt water on any new bush being put in the ground. Gaddy Taylor was in her element, offering paper cups of water to the exhausted workers, with a plate of cookies on the side for energy and sustenance in case they were needed.

Miss Evelyn was there, too, dressed in a sweater and jeans. She was collecting all the discarded burlaps and putting them on Harry Bain's truck to be taken away. "Well, so much for writing letters," Jeb snickered.

He was both amused and nonplussed at the scene being acted out on the hill. Mrs Manning had said something a few weeks ago about wanting to get some more flowering shrubs, and that fall would be the best planting time. Jeb had considered this statement and wondered where in the world she thought she would have room to put them. She explained her plan to him. He just hadn't thought they could fit all that in.

Jeb watched with a smile as wiry, little Mrs. Manning hopped about on the sun dial directing her subjects like an orchestra leader. Daisy was perched on one of the rocks above the lawn, safely out of the way. She was not going to miss a minute of this special performance in her front yard, but not about to get anywhere near the cistern or the water hose Carter was slinging around, either.

For a moment, Jeb simply leaned against a large Sycamore's trunk to watch the show.

A quiet but resonant voice said, "Amanda is in fine fettle, today." Jeb almost jumped out of his skin when he realized George Raven's Wing was standing on the other side of the big tree, watching just as he was.

"Yessuh, it sure looks like it. It surely does," Jeb agreed. The old Indian was leaning against the tree with his arms folded. Jeb thought he could detect a partially hidden smile in the wrinkles of the Crow's face.

He decided he might chance a bit of conversation. "It's mighty nice to see her acting a little spunky again."

"Yes," was the reply. "Among White women, Amanda Manning is strong."

She was waving her arms and pointing, shouting directions to the willing group as if she were leading the Philharmonic, wielding a garden trowel like a baton. Jeb had to give it to her. She was a real piece of work, his Miz Manning was. No doubt about it.

All at once she spotted him. "Jebediah! Oh, Jebediah, I'm so glad you're finally here. Please, come and help me. You know what has to be done. Show these people how to do it. I'm running out of breath."

Jeb started walking toward her. She had handed him the baton and with a shake of his head he stepped into the fray, but not onto the cistern. When he looked back over his shoulder, George Raven's Wing had vanished.

 Chapter Twenty-Seven

They had mostly closed up shop for the winter in the yard, so to speak. After all that collaborative work, the new shrubs were set in and had a hold on. The weather had become threatening and unreliable.

Jeb's mother asked him to go shopping with her to help with the heavier things and the grocery sacks. That kind of duty was kin to doing time in the pokey for Jeb. But he felt he owed her, and some of his afternoons were now free. Actually, she did a little bribing. Jeb had taken Driver's Education at school in the fall and had his license now. She told him he could drive if he came along. That was the clincher. He went fairly willingly. Anything for a chance to get behind the wheel.

Laticia did a little early Christmas shopping first; and Jeb moseyed around the shops hoping to get some ideas of what he might get his family as gifts. They stopped for groceries and ended up in a small used furniture store that carried everything from soup to nuts. Jeb's mother was looking at end tables she wanted to get for the house. Jeb was getting bored out of his gourd.

Suddenly he spied something that caught his interest, practically hidden in a dusty, forgotten corner of the store. Peeking out from behind an old chipped vase was a small picture with a gold oval frame. Carefully he extricated it from its dark perch and looked at it intently. It was a small oil painting of a bowl of yellow, white, and purple Pansies.

The gold leaf frame was dirty and flaking around the edge. But Jeb knew it was exactly what he wanted. He could fix it almost like new. The price was five dollars. He was paying for his prize when his mother came up to the counter.

"What you want that old thing for, Jeb?" she said. Then she bit her tongue and said nothing more. She knew.

When they got home, Jeb carried everything into the house for his mother and went back to the garage.

At his father's workbench, he took great pains to pry the clips from the back of the picture frame and carefully took out the little painting. Intently he inspected it for flaws. Finding none, he set it aside. Thankfully, it was only very dusty.

He found a small piece of fine sandpaper and began to smooth the flaking paint on the wooden frame. Jeb worked slowly and deliberately with the same patience he tended the growing things.

When the frame was smooth enough for his satisfaction, he rummaged in an old basket and came up with a can half full of gold spray paint. Jeb laid the frame on a newspaper and very carefully sprayed the entire surface.

Much to the amusement of his family, he repeated this process several days in a row, allowing the paint to dry thoroughly between each application. His brothers and Naomi ribbed him about making something special for his "old girlfriend". But it was a gentle teasing, so he pretty much ignored them.

When the frame looked almost new, Jeb rubbed it with fine steel wool, painted a thin coat of colorless lacquer on it and let it dry. He then took the painting and wiped it with a slightly dampened clean rag, then with a cloth barely moistened with linseed oil he had found on the workbench.

When cleaned up, the Pansies looked bright and sparkling, almost real. Their dainty "faces" seemed to be smiling out at him, bringing a genuine smile to his own face as those little flowers always did.

After the painting was again securely clipped to the refurbished wooden oval, Jeb's mother found just the right size box to fit it. He folded tissue paper around it, put it in the box, and wrapped it in green Christmas paper with red and white Poinsettias on it. His special gift remained on the closet shelf in his room, ready and waiting.

# Chapter Twenty-Eight

When Mrs. Manning arrived at Jeb's house one evening the week before Christmas, the whole family was excited and greetings were profuse. Privately, Jeb fretted about her because it became dark so early. He had witnessed her driving as mighty suspect in broad daylight, and he figured it ought to be double dangerous at night.

She had brought them all the usual treats she made every year, but this time she had added a fruitcake she said was her specialty. Jeb didn't want to tell her that fruitcake was definitely not his favorite. Actually, he rated it just a notch above spinach.

Mrs. Manning brought another gift for the whole family; four big bags of tulip bulbs. She apologized for bringing them so late in the year, but said she had ordered them from a catalogue because they were such rare and beautiful colors, and they had just arrived. "Don't tell Felix, please, Jebediah. He'd think I was disloyal." Jeb only chuckled.

"Jebediah will know what to do and how to plant them," she said proudly. "They may not bloom this spring when planted so late, but your family can enjoy them every year thereafter."

Jeb's mother was especially delighted and knew immediately the spot where she wanted to put them. Laticia had made some spiced pumpkin bread which she knew Mrs. Manning had a hankering for. Mrs. Manning thanked her, saying how much she adored pumpkin bread, and groaning that she'd probably gain five pounds. Everybody laughed picturing little Mrs. Manning fatter.

This time she had brought Jeb lots of books. *Lord, she must think I'm a Einstein or something*, he worried. There was another book on growing things, NATIVE FLOWERS AND TREES OF KANSAS. A large dictionary and thesaurus, which she said was for college. Lord knew he hoped he'd get there. She also gave him a small pocket dictionary, and with a twinkle in her eye said she thought maybe his other one was worn out by now. He hadn't even known she knew about his old one. Laughing, he thanked her kindly. You had to hand it to her. She was a sharp ol' buzzard, his Miz Manning.

She was gathering up her empty box and her purse preparing to leave, when Jeb touched her shoulder gently and handed her his gift. Her eyes widened in surprise. "For me?" she said.

"Yessum," he answered softly.

"I'm so surprised and pleased, Jebediah. May I open it now?" she eagerly slipped the paper from the package without waiting for his answer. He nodded, pleased that she seemed so anxious and praying she would like it.

When she saw what was in the package, Mrs. Manning began to look hurriedly for her glasses. She rummaged through her purse, felt in her pockets. The family began to smile and Naomi started to giggle. "What in the world have I done with my glasses?" she exclaimed impatiently.

Naomi stepped up to her pointing. "They on top of your head, Miz Manning!" Laticia pulled her back, chiding her but everybody laughed anyway.

"Oh my, yes, of course. That's where they usually are and I always forget them." She arranged them carefully on her nose, then took the little painting from the box. She peered intently at it for several seconds while Jeb held his breath. "Oh, Jebediah, Jebediah! It's such a perfect gift, I shall treasure it always," she said looking at him with tears in her eyes.

Jeb had such a lump in his throat he couldn't say anything, so he kept on smiling at her. He realized that he had chosen well. All that work had been worth it for this moment. His eyes began to sting a little bit. He chanced a look at his family and saw they were all standing around, grinning like idiots. It eased him some not to be the only fool.

 *Chapter Twenty-Nine*

J eb's family had a wonderful Christmas that year. He had asked his mother if he could hold a little out of his pay back to buy presents for the family. She thought it was a grand idea and was proud of him. He found a skinny black doll that sort of looked like a Barbie doll. Lots of silly, frilly clothes came with it. It was mighty expensive. Jeb reckoned he ought to save up to buy stock in a doll factory and maybe get rich at those prices. He asked his brothers, Eli and Jerry, to go in with him to buy it for Naomi. Jeb figured the three of them could handle it. The boys doled out happily, grateful for any idea for their private little pest. That dumb doll and been a real success. Naomi was crazy about it.

Jeb gave Eli a sweatshirt that had BIG BRO' printed in large letters across the front. Eli had laughed, delighted, and whacked him one on top of the head.

Jerry got a book of gift certificates for McDonald's because that's were he always loved to get hamburgers. Jerry's eyes lit up like a Christmas tree when he opened that present; and Jeb felt he had done exactly the right thing.

Jeb bought a small, reasonably priced tool box for his Dad on sale at the hardware store. It had a plastic liner molded to hold pliers, a hammer, screw drivers, a metal ruler, and several small wrenches. Pop had smiled real big when he opened it and gave him a bear hug, which Jeb took to mean he liked it a lot.

Jeb thought Momma had been a lot harder to buy for. She was more particular about things she really liked, kind of like Miz Manning. He finally decided on a little china vase with different col-ored ceramic flowers on it. She had wiped away a few happy tears when she opened it, and told him how beautiful she thought it was. But she did that over everything her children gave her. Then she had put it right out in plain view on one of her new end tables, and cau-tioned everyone to be careful of her prized possession. She dusted it faithfully every day.

Jeb had made out right well, himself, with gifts his family gave him. His folks bought him some new shirts for school, the kind that looked nice but you didn't have to tuck them in. He liked those best. They gave him a new wallet and a bunch of socks, a most welcome gift, because he had worn holes in most of his old ones, Eli's too, because Jerry's socks were still too small for him.

Eli and Jerry gave him a black baseball cap with JEBEDIAH in gold letters on it. They told him they thought he needed a new one because the old one was such a dilapidated disgrace. He knew it was their idea of a joke. Even so, he laughed and thanked them. He put it away thinking he might never wear it.

Jeb seemed to have gained a new and well deserved confidence and self esteem. He even bought a gold enameled Mickey Mouse charm for the bracelet he had seen Cordelia wear. She acted thrilled and her eyes had sparkled a lot.

He got up his nerve and asked her to the Holiday dance. She accepted! Jeb felt like walking on air.

 *Chapter Thirty*

Winter was finally fizzling out and Jeb was elated. He could hardly wait to see if their Azaleas had survived the cold weather. Besides, he hadn't seen Mrs. Manning since Christmastime and he was anxious to see how she had weathered, also.

Early one Saturday morning during his first walk up the hill, Jeb did the usual assessment of possible freeze damage. When he looked toward the house, he saw her. Lord, no matter what he did, he couldn't get ahead of Miz Manning. She was already out messing around in the yard. She greeted him heartily and immediately dragged him around to the front yard. Daisy followed, begging for his attention. Jeb picked her up and carried her along scratching her gently and talking softly in her ear. The cat felt heavier to him. He thought maybe she was getting a little older and putting on winter weight.

"Look, Jebediah. Carter gave me some white elephants for Christmas." Jeb had no idea what she was talking about because on either side of the front walk reposed cement lions with cement baskets on their backs.

"I don't see white elephants anywhere, Miz Manning, just those lions," he said puzzled.

She laughed and laughed. "Oh, mercy me, I forgot what an innocent you are, Jebediah. A reference to a white elephant sometimes means something you don't know what to do with."

"Yessum, I see." But he didn't. He put Daisy on the ground and she immediately jumped into the "basket" atop one of the "elephant" lions.

"I can't get rid of them, you understand, because they were a gift from my son; but I've never really cared for lions at all. I guess the joke's on me and I'm just stuck with them." Mrs. Manning chuckled again and shook her head smiling.

"Don't you dare tell Carter about our predicament, Jebediah. Cross your heart and hope to kiss a pickle."

Jeb wagged his head back and forth and stated positively, "No, Ma'am! I swear I won't do that."

"We'll just have to fill them with flowers and make the best of it. Red and white Geraniums ought to do the trick. We'll call them our sentimental sentinels."

"Yessum," he said, still not quite understanding the joke. He thought those concrete lions looked sort of regal sitting there staring out into space. Lord knew he'd seen lots worse stuff sitting in other folks' yards.

"Jebediah, get in the car. We'll go out to Felix Dalgren's and get enough Geraniums to camouflage those beasts right away," Mrs. Manning said determinedly.

Holy Moly! Jeb panicked. *Not the car first thing off!*

"Miz Manning, why don't you go on out to get the Geraniums and I'll just get started here in the yard?"

"Don't be silly, Jebediah. Hiding those white elephants is much more important. And I'll need your help picking out the best plants and getting them in the car," she stated. "The yard can wait."

"Yessum." Resignedly, Jeb walked slowly to the car like a condemned man.

It was another harrowing ride, just as Jeb expected; but they eventually made it. Hopefully she'd do another snail ride home with all her new Geranium "pets" in the back.

Felix came lumbering out to greet them. But Mrs. Manning was on a tear and already heading for the rows on rows of Geraniums.

"Morning, Jebediah. What's Mandy Lil up to today?"

"Morning, Mister Felix. I think she's fixin' to try and hide some white elephants."

"That so?" said a puzzled Mr. Dalgren who followed Mandy Lil around the seas of plants. It took an hour or more for Felix and Beulah to aid them in picking out just the right plants to suit Mrs. Manning. When it came to her flowers, Mrs. Manning was particular as all get out.

The slow ride back was without incident; and a relieved Jeb unloaded the trunk of the car. Nobody could say life around Miz Manning was dull.

He worked for an hour unpotting and planting, adding new soil, peat, and "magic elixir". Mrs. Manning directed and fussed around the whole time, pinching off dead leaves and stacking the empty pots. It took her quite a while with Daisy's help because she had to do it over again several times when the cat playfully knocked over the stacks.

"There!" she said triumphantly when they were finished. "That's the best we can do. With the white ones edging the baskets and the red ones in the center, the eye is drawn immediately to the red blossoms and lingers not on the basket-bearing beasts."

"Yessum," Jeb said, "Just so long as you're satisfied."

"Well, I have to be, don't I? Oh, I almost forgot. Come into the house with me for a moment, please, Jebediah. There's something I want you to see."

This surprised him greatly since he had never before been inside Mrs. Manning's home. But he followed willingly as she lead him through the living room, down the hall and into her bedroom. She pointed to the corner on the other side of her bed. There stood a tall, narrow chest with multiple small drawers, and above it hung the painting of the Pansies.

Jeb was dumbstruck. Slowly, he moved toward the corner for a closer look. He put his hands on top of the chest and leaned in near the painting. He wanted to make sure the gold frame he had painted was holding up and the flowers still looked fresh and not dusty. To him it seemed wonderful and a lump came to his throat thinking she had put it here in this special place.

"I wanted you to see how much your gift means to me, Jebediah. Those are the flowers we both love so much because they make us feel happy. I hung them there so I can see them each morning when I wake up and start the day with a smile."

When he trusted himself to speak, he said quietly, "That's nice, Miz Manning. That's real nice. I'm real glad it pleases you."

As they walked back down the hall, she said, "I need to ask a favor of you, if you will, Jebediah. There's a large coffee table here in the living room. It's too heavy for me to move by myself, and I want it situated in front of that sofa across the room."

"Good as done, Miz Manning. Good as done," Jeb said as he went quickly to the table. Mrs. Manning came over to assist him.

"Now, it's my turn to do the bossing, Miz Manning. You got no cause to fool around with somethin' so heavy. You just set down, now, you hear. My back is strong enough for both of us," Jeb stated authoritatively.

"Yes, Sir!" she replied and sat while he effortlessly moved the table.

Outside, they worked for another hour, each delighted to discover big, healthy buds on the Azaleas. The two of them had danced around like excited kids. At noon, Mrs. Manning made sandwiches which they ate on the porch because they wanted to look at the Azaleas, as if they expected them to burst into bloom at any minute right in front of their eyes.

Mrs. Manning said she felt rather tired and was going in to rest. Jeb worked a few hours longer and then headed home.

His grades at school had continued to improve. *Just a matter of concentrating harder*, Jeb thought. His folks were thrilled and extremely proud. Now, he felt he might make it to graduation in better shape than he had hoped for. He was pleased, himself, more than he cared to admit.

Cordelia had agreed to go with him to the Senior Prom in May. Mrs. Manning had been right again. With a little courage and a bit of time, he had Cordelia had become good friends. In fact, he more than liked her and he thought she was a little sweet on him, too. Leastways, he hoped so. Things were really looking up for Jeb. Life was good.

Chapter Thirty-One

The next time Jeb went to Mrs. Manning's, Billy was there. He told Jeb she had taken cookies to his house at Christmastime, too. Jeb thought that was nice; but Billy hadn't said anything about books or tulips or Mrs. Manning's special sugared pecans. Neither of them had seen or heard of Hack for about six months.

They worked together the rest of the afternoon getting the vegetable garden ready for planting and the beds prepared for the annual plants. Mrs. Manning must have been out with her "girls" because they didn't see her.

When Jeb arrived for work later in the week, Mrs. Manning was practically hopping with glee. The Azaleas were in full bloom. Jeb was almost as excited as she was, and proud as a peacock.

It had started to warm up quite a bit, and as she pulled at a few weeds, Mrs. Manning felt suddenly faint. Jeb happened to look up as she staggered a little and was at her side like a shot.

"I don't know what's the matter with me, Jebediah. I felt so dizzy all at once," she murmured weakly.

Jeb supported her weight easily and, lifting her gently, carried her to the recliner on the porch. "Rest here a minute, Miz Manning. I'm gonna run in and get you a drink of water."

He raced into the kitchen and being completely unfamiliar with the room, frantically opened four or five cabinets before he finally found a glass and filled it with water. He hurried back to the porch and watched worriedly as she sipped.

"Miz Manning, I think I ought to call Mister Carter to come," Jeb said.

"No! No, Jebediah. That's not necessary. I'm fine, now, really. It was just a little spell. I've had them before. It's passed now. It's merely one of the inconveniences of getting older."

He wasn't so sure, because she looked like she'd been whitewashed. But he didn't want to go against her wishes, so he sat quietly beside her and watched as she rested. Soon she got up and said she thought she'd go in and lie down for a bit, as a precaution. Jeb helped her into the house and told her to call out to him if she needed anything.

He went on working because he didn't know what else to do; but he kept looking up at the house every now and again. He was relieved to see Miss Evelyn drive up at her usual time. He waved at her as she went into the house. Jeb knew if anything was amiss with Miz Manning, Miss Evelyn would know what to do.

He was surprised after Mister Carter arrived some time later to see Miz Manning come out on the porch with Miss Evelyn, who was carrying a tray with cookies and drinks for all of them.

Jeb was watching closely. Miz Manning had a little color in her cheeks and didn't look quite so ghosty. He didn't know whether she'd told either Miss Evelyn or Mister Carter about her little "spell". But he thought he ought not to be the one to spill the beans, so he held his peace.

They were quietly munching and sipping when Mrs. Manning broke the comfortable silence. "We went to Europe on our honeymoon," she said dreamily.

Jeb and Carter looked at each other. Jeb thinking she might have slipped a cog in her dizziness. Carter wondering at the reason for the non sequitur.

But Mrs. Manning knew exactly what she about. She was simply continuing the story of her life where they had tabled it last fall.

"England first, then France and Belgium, Germany and Austria. It was a perfect honeymoon, the most wonderful anyone could have ever wished for. The time was before the second World War, you see, and the aura and romance of Europe was never to be equaled again. Of course, I could speak with everyone and that was so helpful," she said proudly. The men nodded in agreement, knowing this was absolutely the truth.

"When we returned to the United States, there was no actual settling down, as one would think in the usual sense. For several years we led the life of itinerant nomads." Jeb wished he could take out his dictionary without looking like a dummy. "We'd live a year here, a

year there, with my husband overseeing the management of many of
the branch newspapers. Even two years in South America. That was
exciting, so different from our lives in this country. An entirely different culture."

"Then Carter came along, much to our delight; and our lives were
definitely turned upside down, having a little one under foot. The
three of us became a real family then, and settled more nearly into
that kind of lifestyle." She looked lovingly at her son.

"Carter, you were such a joy and always have been. You've made
me and your father very proud."

Jeb didn't like the way she sounded, like she was on her last legs
and making a deathbed confession. So he said quietly, "Miz Manning,
when did you get all those writing awards framed on the wall down at
the paper?"

"Oh, that! Well, those happened almost by accident, Jebediah,"
she smiled happily. She seemed to have perked up a bit. "The three
of us moved back here to Valleyville after Carter's grandfather passed
away. Carter went to high school here and we built this house two
years before he graduated. With a nearly grown son, church work,
bridge games and gardening didn't seem fulfilling enough. I was casting about for something ambitious to do. That's when my husband
suggested I try a weekly column. At first I thought the idea sounded
absurd; but then it finally grew on me, so I made an attempt." Mrs.
Manning shook her head reflecting.

Carter, enjoying the recounting, interrupted to tell Evelyn and Jeb
that her column had been a huge success from the get-go. She had
written chattily about interesting townspeople, about some of her
friends, on humorous events that happened in the family, and sometimes, her views on important issues. People loved it; and his mother
had always downplayed her popularity. Evelyn had never heard any of
this and was fascinated with the story.

"When I received my first writing award, my husband nearly fell
off his chair in shock. That really delighted me because I think he was
just trying to keep me busy and never dreamed my work would be
noticed for any kind of award recognition," she laughed aloud,
remembering the look on her husband's face. Jeb smiled, too,

pleased to see her become more animated.

"As my writing became more widely recognized, the awards kept coming from time to time. Every other year or so. I was actually as amazed as anyone. I began to wonder who the Judges were for these things. It seemed to me that some of what I considered my best work was overlooked, and I was given merit for some of what I thought of as my so-so writing. Eventually, I stopped trying to figure it out, just thanked everybody, and kept writing in my own style, for my own pleasure."

"Good for you! I'm impressed," Evelyn said sincerely.

Jeb was happy that he had finally learned the story of how she came to write; but he thought she looked kind of tuckered out. So he thanked them and said his good-byes, declined a ride from Carter, and walked home, smiling and remembering.

Late that night, at three o'clock in the morning, the police came to his house and took him to jail in handcuffs.

 *Chapter Thirty-Two*

PAIN! It coursed through Mrs. Manning's body in huge waves. Dull and aching, sharp and throbbing. Pain encompassed her whole body so intensely she couldn't define it or locate the source. Even taking a shallow breath caused her agony.

She opened her eyes, only barely, another painful process. The lids seemed stuck together. Everything looked gray and blurred.

I've lost my glasses again, she thought inanely. Slowly her vision focused more clearly. Everything seemed whiter; and she was aware of a light above her head. She wondered if she'd died and was in heaven...or hell, maybe. She didn't think one was supposed to hurt so much in heaven.

Gradually, she became aware of someone at her side. She was astonished to realize she was in bed.

Carter looked down at his mother with grateful tears in his eyes. "Mother, you're back with us again. I'm so glad. We thought we'd lost you," he choked out in a rasping voice.

"Carter?" her voice was not much more than a hoarse whisper. She hardly recognized the sound as coming from herself. It sounded as if she was deep in a well.

"Wh...where am I, son? What happened to me?" The effort to speak was so great it very nearly exhausted her.

Devastated, Carter stared at his pitiful little mother. She was a mass of deep, purple bruises, her eyes almost swollen shut, cuts on her face and arms. He was filled with an anger and frustration so deep it almost paralyzed him.

That day on the porch, he had thought she looked so pale, he had stopped later in the evening to check on her. He found her unconscious on the floor in the living room. He was certain she was dead. Blood was splattered everywhere. It was evident she had hit her head on the coffee table when she fell, or more likely, was slammed to the floor. The house had been ransacked. Most of her jewelry was gone, along with all the silver. Priceless vases and fig-urines were broken. Contents of drawers were scattered throughout the house. Her purse had been emptied and her car stolen.

Theses facts he hadn't learned until much later. He had gone with her to the hospital in the ambulance. Because it was a break-in and an assault, the 911 people had alerted the police who came even before the ambulance attendants could stabilize his mother and trans-port her.

All of that seemed insignificant in view of her battered and tenu-ous condition. She had barely been breathing. His fear for her almost overcame him. He was completely enraged that anyone could com-mit such a despicable act.

That had been five days ago and she had been in a coma ever since. He gazed at her now with such love and pity, he could barely respond. "Mother, you're in the hospital. You were badly beaten. You have lots of cuts and bruises. The doctors say you are healing, and they think you'll be fine after a time." But she had already lapsed into a sedated sleep, and he was glad she could escape the pain.

He hadn't told her that several ribs were broken, that she had a severely sprained shoulder and ankle. Doctors told him it was a mira-cle there weren't more broken bones. The police said the same thing, considering the evidence of the violence at the scene.

Carter didn't know when, if ever, he would tell her about her car and jewelry and the wreck at the house. That seemed a small conse-quence if only she survived. She was a tough little cookie, his mother, and he loved her dearly. So he sat down at her bedside again, and with his head in his hands, waited and prayed.

Chapter Thirty-Three

This critically dangerous time for his mother and the events that had accompanied her assault had drained Carter emotionally and physically. He was completely exhausted. He had remained by her bedside almost constantly. After the first few days of Mrs. Manning's coma, Evelyn or Gaddy took turns sitting at her side, to give Carter a brief respite from his vigil at least once a day.

The night they had taken Mrs. Manning into the hospital emergency room, Carter had called Evelyn to go to the house and see what she could do to help.

She had been aghast at the situation and more than willing to offer her assistance in any way she could. The police were still collecting evidence and dusting for fingerprints and wouldn't let her do anything.

They had found Daisy behind the couch unconscious. At first they thought she was dead and brought her to Evelyn, who detected a faint heartbeat. She called the vet's emergency number and took the cat to him immediately, in spite of the late hour. He had diagnosed a coma from a concussion, and also broken ribs. Evelyn would later learn that Daisy had suffered a similar fate and resulting condition to Mrs. Manning's.

The vet and Evelyn could only surmise that the cat had attempted to come to her mistress' rescue by attacking the intruder and been bashed against the wall for her efforts.

The animal doctor suggested that Evelyn leave the cat with him for however long it took for her recuperation. He thought Daisy might make it, but he couldn't say definitely.

Evelyn had gone back to the house, disregarding the time. The forensics officers had finished with what they could do inside, and allowed her stay to lock up.

She had then proceeded to the hospital to be with Carter. He was completely distraught. The doctors were still fighting to keep his mother alive and trying to ascertain the extent of all her injuries.

Carter remembered leaving the hospital the next afternoon at the urging of the doctors. His mother was still in a coma but alive, and had been taken to Intensive Care at dawn. Carter had sat beside her bed almost constantly for six hours. There was no change in her condition.

He had made several calls; one to the newspaper to apprise them of what had happened and let them know he wouldn't be in until he knew something definite. The other call he made to Gaddy Taylor, who was beside herself with distress, hearing what happened to Mrs. Manning. He asked her, please, to go to the house and clean up some of the ransacked mess. Evelyn called the Post Office and told them she wouldn't be there because of the emergency, and offered to go to the house and help Gaddy. After all, she had seen it earlier and knew restoring any kind of order was going to be a job for more than one person.

Carter left the hospital about two o'clock and went home to shower, shave, and change clothes. He made a phone call to the police from his mother's house at about three.

Carter spoke rapidly into the phone. "Buck, it's Carter. I think maybe you had better come up here to Mother's place to check something out."

Buck Thompson had been the Chief of Police in Valleyville for a number of years. He was very popular with the townspeople and had been re-elected, with the public's strong vote of confidence in his abilities, several times. He and Carter had been good friends ever since they were in school together, and also because police business was of great interest to the newspaper.

"What's up now, Carter? More bad news?" Thompson had caught the note of urgency in Manning's voice. He knew Carter was going through a terrible ordeal in the aftermath of his mother's beating and wasn't even sure whether or not she would live. Buck, as well as the entire town, was outraged by the senseless battery of the well respected older woman. His men on the force were trying to wrap up the case against that Jenkins boy as quickly as possible and his sympathies were solidly with his friend, Carter.

"Nothing more to report on Mother's condition, Buck. They still don't know anything definite. It's just touch and go, but I'm hopeful. Anyway, I came over to Mother's this afternoon to help Gaddy and Evelyn try to get some sense of order back in the house, since your crew was through here. As I drove up the hill, I saw something very strange. The sun dial is off the top of the cistern. This has never happened before and it would take more than one person to lift that granite block. Thought I ought to call you first before I went down there, in case it had something to do with the robbery and I might mess up some evidence before you could take a look at it."

"Right, Carter. Good thinking. We'll be out there just as soon as I can get a couple of my boys together," the Chief said gravely. "Don't let anybody go near it before we arrive, and thanks, Carter."

The Chief and two men came with the Crime Lab van very soon after the phone call. They were on the lawn around the cistern taking samples of the ground and checking for footprints or tracks of any kind. It was obvious, as Carter had said, that one person couldn't have moved that sun dial alone. It would have taken two or more. Therefore, if this had any relation to the robbery, there would have to have been at least one accomplice.

While they waited for the men to complete their evidence gathering, Buck told Carter how far along they were in investigating the case. He said they were pretty sure that Jeb Jenkins did it, and they had him in custody.

Carter was dumfounded. "Buck, I know you know your job; but in this instance, I think you're way off course. I know that kid. He would never do something like this."

"Yeah, we all think we know somebody until something like this happens. You'd be surprised what some seemingly nice people will do. I think you're dead wrong. We have too much concrete evidence against him," Buck said doggedly.

Carter was overwhelmed with this information. "Let me go down to the jail and talk with the boy. Maybe that would clear things up."

"That wouldn't be a very wise move, under the circumstances, Carter. In fact, I advise against it. If he is guilty, and we're pretty sure he is; and if, God forbid, your mother doesn't survive, we're looking at murder here," Buck stated bluntly and Carter flinched. "Your talking to him could only confuse the issue and make him think he has an out with your sympathy. Don't do it, guy."

A shocked Carter nodded defeatedly and went to the immediate problem. "That cistern is deeper than most any I have ever heard of," he revealed. "That's why my Dad had it capped and the dial put on top. We'll never know what might be down there unless we get some experienced divers to go down to reconnoiter."

"Then that's what we'll do as soon as we cover the ground around it for evidence." Buck went back to the squad car, parked on the side of the driveway, and called the station.

"It'll take them at least a couple of hours to get some divers rounded up. We'll have to rely on those boys who do a lot of diving for the Corps of Engineers over at Lake Benton. They're the only ones with enough experience we have access to around here. Diving isn't the most popular sport in the middle of Kansas," he said wryly. "I'm going to leave a man here to guard the area and we'll just have to wait. I'll be back when we get somebody."

It took five hours to get two divers to the scene. It had become dark. Carter wanted to get back to the hospital to check on his mother; but he had a hunch this was vitally important. He called the hospital and was told there was no change, so he decided to stay put and see what resulted.

It was pitch black by the time the men were suited up and had hooked up a generator for adequate lighting.

Buck and Carter both had the old legend of the haunted cistern in the back of their minds. They had heard the story told over and over again since they were children growing up together. Neither said a word, but each felt a little uneasy none the less. They were grown men and certainly didn't believe in ghosts; but the lore would not dispel itself from their thinking.

At this point curiosity got the best of Evelyn and a reluctant Gaddy and they joined the men gathered around the black hole in the middle of the lawn, as divers began the descent. There was total quiet among the onlookers.

The Crime Lab men were waiting in case there was evidence to examine. Several policemen were also there to help secure the area from possible inquisitive thrill-seekers.

As the divers went deeper into the cistern on the heavy ropes they had thrown over the side, their voices took on an unearthly sound, making the atmosphere seem even spookier.

"There's a kind of ledge down here a few feet above the water, Chief," one of the divers yelled up to the waiting group. His voice echoed in the cavernous dark, adding an even more eerie aura to the scene. "We see some bags or something on the part that sticks out the farthest."

"Can you bring them up?" Buck shouted into the darkness. "We'll try," came the faint reply.

At that moment, called by a premonition, a huge man walked out of the night into their midst. Gaddy gave out a piercing scream, startling them all. Everyone jumped as if he were shot and the officers reached for their weapons.

"Hold it, boys!" Carter recognized George Raven's Wing as he stood in the lights beside the hollow depths.

The tall figure loomed above them in the temporary illumination which hung on a stake in the ground. His large, craggy features were in half shadow, giving him a spectral appearance. The group stood in hushed silence, gaping.

Suddenly, a black figure emerged at the opening in the ground. The diver carried a big sack on his back. This made it awkward for him to get over the side, so an officer took the burden from him. As the man stood erect, he saw Raven's Wing. Flabbergasted by the sight, he stepped quickly backward and nearly fell back into the cistern. Buck grasped his arm to steady him.

A voice from the deep hole yelled urgently. "There's a bunch of bones on the ledge down here under these bags!"

George Raven's Wing stepped toward the edge of the cistern and, raising his arms, began to chant in the ancient language of his Crow Tribe. The group around him was spellbound.

Another black-suited figure began to crawl over the edge of the well. He hauled two sacks. The crime lab men stepped close enough to take the bags from him. He stumbled from the dark lip of the hole and saw the chanting Indian above him. He let out a yelp and sidled away into the darkness on all fours. The Crow lowered his arms, breaking the spell. Everyone began to laugh nervously. Extreme edginess and tension had gained an enormous hold on them all.

One of the criminal investigators had immediately taken the first haul to the mobile lab to view its contents. He called from the van, "Chief, this sack is full of silver. Trays, coffee pots, stuff like that."

"That has to be Mother's silver service," Carter said. "All the silver was stolen."

"What do you want to do about them bones?" said the first diver.

To a person, they all looked to George Raven's Wing questioningly.

The big man stared off into the night. The rest waited silently, respectfully, not daring to breathe.

"I wish to take my Grandfather home to our people. Now, his spirit may find peace and rest. It is over."

It took Carter, Evelyn and Gaddy quite a while to find a suitable receptacle in which to place the bones of George's ancestor. A large, hard-sided, battered suitcase, found in the garage, was finally decided upon.

The reluctant divers were eventually persuaded to retrieve the remains of the skeleton. Raven's Wing chanted over every bone as it was placed into the suitcase. Carter offered to take the Indian home but he refused. He closed the case with great ceremony and reverence and disappeared with it into the night. His life-long mission was ending.

He had told Carter that he came tonight because his Grandfather's spirit had called to him. Carter again felt shivers down his spine. After nearly a full century, the old man had fulfilled his singular, self-imposed quest.

The police had stayed to secure the area. Officers painstakingly hammered the heavy wooden lid tightly on the cistern and fitted the leaden granite sun dial in place on top of it. The divers removed all their gear and the lighting. Crime Lab men left to continue their job of finding possible evidence. Later, the final report from them was that no fingerprints were found on any of the silver pieces which were badly mangled from the long drop into the cistern.

The police would now question the Jenkins boy intensively to find out who his accomplice or accomplices were.

Chapter Thirty-Four

Consciousness came to Mrs. Manning once again later in that same day, five days into the aftermath of her ordeal. The pain was stronger, but her mind seemed less muddled. Some of what had happened that dreadful night was slowly seeping back into her memory. She cringed inwardly with the knowledge.

Carter tried his best to smile at her. "Welcome back, Mother," he said softly. "Hello," she croaked.

Vaguely she remembered answering the door, thinking it might be Carter. But the person she recognized on the porch was angry and menacing, forcing his way past her into the house. She had protested loudly, but he twisted her arm painfully behind her back and shoved her before him down the hall towards her bedroom. She was locked in his painful grip and deeply afraid. As he raked through her jewelry chest, she had wrenched herself free and run to the living room, hoping to reach the telephone. There, he had overtaken her and slapped her hard across the face, causing her to fall to the floor, hitting her head on the table in front of the sofa. She must have lost consciousness for a while, but came to some time later. From the floor she woozily viewed broken lamps, figurines and vases.

He was still there; and to her horror was putting her beautiful silver into a gunnysack.

She had tried to sit up as he was emptying her purse. The contents tumbled down upon her. When he saw she was again conscious, he took the large purse and beat her across the face and head. She put up her arms to ward off the blows, but he continued to wield the purse as hard as he could, until the pain was unbearable and blackness engulfed her.

She thought, now, that he must have left her for dead, thinking she could no longer identify him. All these remembered impressions returned to her still fuzzy mind like pictures flashing across a screen.

"Some of it is coming back, Carter," she rasped out.

"I know, Mother, but try not to think about it now. Rest and concentrate on getting well," he said kindly. "The police have him in custody. His fingerprints were all over the house. Jeb will pay for this, Mother. I promise you that."

"Jebediah?" she whispered, puzzled. "What about Jebediah?" She knew something was not right, but she couldn't think clearly. She was very upset and didn't know exactly why.

A nurse came to the other side of the bed with a hypodermic needle. "The doctor says she mustn't become agitated, Mr. Manning. Anyway, it's past time for her sedative for the pain. We need to keep her as calm as possible." Mrs. Manning felt the needle go into her arm.

"No! Carter, please, no!" There was something important she wanted to tell him; but she couldn't remember what it was. Then sleep claimed her once again.

# Chapter Thirty-Five

J eb lay in a fetal position on the hard cot in his jail cell. He was exhausted and frightened to the depths of his being.

The whole household had awakened that night the police took him into custody. His mother had screamed in anguish when they handcuffed him. His father had wanted to follow him down to the jail; but the police wanted to question him and wouldn't let him out of the house.

First thing off they took Jeb's fingerprints. They interrogated him until the sun came up; and he still didn't know why. The questions were all centered around his work at Mrs. Manning's house; how often he worked there, the last time he was there, when he had left. He couldn't make any sense of it and they wouldn't tell him anything.

Then fear gripped his heart. Something had happened to Miz Manning and nobody would tell him.

The following night they had awakened him in his cell and taken him to a brightly lighted room to question him again. This time they wanted to know what he had done with the rest of the jewelry. They told him they had found the silver in the cistern and wanted to know who was in this with him.

He hadn't the slightest notion what they were asking him about. He told them he knew nothing about any silver or jewelry. If he didn't do anything in the first place, how could he have anybody help him do nothing. They were relentless until he finally quit talking at all and they took him back to the cell.

It was several days before his family fully realized how extremely serious the charges against Jeb were. Burglary and aggravated assault with intent to kill. In panic, they hired Amos Barker to defend him.

Barker was a highly respected Black attorney in Valleyville. He specialized in defending young alleged felons. This was the first time he had been retained to defend a young Black man with a clean slate. Not a mark against him anywhere. Barker was stumped. He couldn't bring himself to believe the young lad was guilty; but the evidence against him was compelling.

Amos had talked with Jeb several times. The first time when he told him what had happened to Mrs. Manning, Jeb had cried like a baby. Barker's years of experience with young people told him the look of horror on the boy's face had been genuine. Barker felt almost certain Jeb could not have been the perpetrator of these terrible crimes. But he had no way to prove his gut feeling.

When Jeb was told she might not survive, was actually barely clinging to life, he was inconsolable.

Amos revealed the charges leveled against him. Jeb shook his head in dismay. He was told that Billy and Hack had both been questioned also; but each seemed to have an airtight alibi.

Billy was at home the entire evening, which all his family attested to. Hack said he had borrowed a friend's car and driven to a nearby town to visit his girlfriend. The car's owner and the girlfriend had backed him up.

Jeb had gone to the movies that night. Cordelia couldn't go with him because she had to study for a test. He said he didn't remember seeing anyone he knew at the show, who could say that he'd been there.

Jeb's fingerprints were all over the house; in the bedroom, on the jewelry chest, on the coffee table where Mrs. Manning hit her head, and all over the kitchen, which was wrecked like the rest of the house. Jeb had tried to explain how and when they got there; but the police didn't believe him.

As was routine, Jeb's attorney asked that he be released on bond until the trial. Because of Mrs. Manning's civic prominence and popularity, the whole town was in an uproar over the crime committed against her. The presiding judge denied bail until after the hearing, reasoning that it would be safer for the boy to be incarcerated temporarily, considering the public's indignation. Jeb's family was outraged. Privately, Amos Barker deemed it a good call.

The known facts seemed to paint a very dark picture for Jeb. He was confused, deeply wounded, and filled with despair.

Chapter Thirty-Six

Mrs. Manning drifted in and out of a dream-like state for almost a week after she first regained consciousness.

Many of her friends came to visit. She had known them, of course, and tried to smile and make a few responses; but the shocked looks on their faces when they saw her depressed her deeply and she was glad when they left.

She knew why they reacted that way. Once when they left her alone she had sneaked a look at her reflection in the bottom of her stainless steel spit pan. She didn't recognize the woman whose ugly face looked back at her. The bruises had turned olive green and baby poop yellow. She appeared to herself like an Asian gargoyle. She didn't acknowledge the dirty, matted, wig-thing atop her head.

Each of her visitors had mentioned that she should never have hired that boy to work for her. She had agreed with them whole-heartedly.

The pain had receded somewhat to a dull ache. She felt like a battered pair of old shoes with hurting feet still in them. She had told them she didn't want so much pain killer, but they kept using her for a pin cushion anyway. Mrs. Manning thought maybe she'd have to get her school teacher voice back and try to stop them. That's what she'd do when she felt a little better, she vowed to herself.

The room looked different. She thought they must have moved her out of Intensive Care. Maybe that was a good sign. She had to have been catnapping when they did it because she couldn't remember. She couldn't keep track of the days or the nights, either one. Time seemed to be blended into one, endlessly painful stretch. She had no idea how long she had been here. A week? A month? She couldn't have said.

She realized Carter was no longer there every time she woke up. She knew that sometimes Gaddy or Evelyn sat beside her, but she rarely spoke to them, merely smiled, acknowledging their presence.

But Carter came every afternoon and evening and she felt better, safer, when he was there.

Something was niggling at her in the back of her mind like Crappies picking at the bait...something crucial she needed to tell him. She had tried to bring it up; but she always seemed to fall asleep on the brink of remembering what it was.

"I must be like Scarlett O'Hara," she chuckled. "I'll think about that tomorrow."

They got her up each day, now, to sit for a while in a chair. It was an extremely painful ordeal; but they said it would help her regain her strength more rapidly.

What strength? she wondered wearily. Whatever strength she had possessed seemed to have been completely lost in the shuffle.

Sitting in the chair contemplating what had happened to her and what might be in store for her, she came to the realization that not only had she been beaten and robbed, she was stripped of human dignity and devalued as an individual.

Mrs. Manning was filled with self pity. She wanted to weep, but she didn't have the energy to do so.

Chapter Thirty-Seven

One week later, Carter came very early, surprising her. "Good morning, Mother. I have good news," he kissed her cheek.

Mrs. Manning was sitting in the chair, feeling more chipper than usual. She had refused her morning sedative, having found at least a semblance of her authoritative school teacher voice. The nurse evidently realized she would brook no nonsense and left her be. Mrs. Manning was sure they would tell on her to her doctor. *Well, maybe I'll be up to handling him, too*, she mentally boasted.

"You're no longer a medical patient, Mother; so today we are taking you to the Valleyville Nursing Facility in order for you to improve enough to go home," Carter stated, pleased.

"But, Carter," she wailed, dismayed, "I want to go home now!"

"I realize that, Mother, and it's what I want for you, too. But that's just not possible right now. You aren't quite strong enough yet. You need some first-class rehabilitation therapy before you can be at home by yourself," Carter explained.

"Well then, I guess I have no choice in the matter, have I?" said his very disappointed mother. "Perhaps getting out of here will be the first step in escape." She laughed cynically.

Preparations for her ride in the ambulance tired her greatly. She had fought like a wild cat when they tried to give her a shot. Carter had finally waved them away, thinking she'd be more upset if they persisted.

Eventually they got her loaded into the ambulance and battened down. "Like a bag of old bones," she had moaned. Carter was riding beside her, talking quietly, trying to soothe her and keep her as calm as possible.

"This will only be a short ride, Mother. We hope it will be a short period of recuperation, also. We'll get someone to stay with you for a while after you go home, until you get used to doing for yourself again," he paused a moment, thinking she might be sleeping. Then he continued speaking normally.

"The authorities seem to have done their best with the investigation. I was so stunned to think that he could possibly do such a thing. I tried several times to go down to the jail and talk to the boy, myself, but the police advised against it. They seem to think they have an airtight case against him. His fingerprints were all over the house."

"That's odd," whispered Mrs. Manning, her eyes half closed, "I thought he wore dark leather gloves. It hurt so when he hit me."

Carter went on talking as if he hadn't heard her. "They seem to know what they're about, and the worst was finding some of your jewelry in his car. Fortunately, they are not trying to drag this thing out and are proceeding rather quickly. The hearing is set at the courthouse for this morning. They're absolutely certain Jeb will be indicted and bound over for trial."

Suddenly, full comprehension flooded Mrs. Manning's brain. A look of sheer horror came to her face. She became very agitated and tried desperately to sit up, but the restraining straps across the stretcher on which she was lying prevented that. She struggled with them impatiently, muttering and keening like a child.

The attendant riding with her glanced at Mr. Manning and prepared to give her an injection. With a strength born of surging adrenaline, Mrs. Manning shrieked "NO!", and flung out her arm, knocking the hypodermic needle out of the paramedic's hand to the floor of the vehicle.

"Turn around! Turn this thing around!" she wailed. "I want to go to the courthouse!" Carter, seriously concerned, shook his head at the driver, who was dumfounded by the commotion.

Mrs. Manning grabbed a startled Carter by the lapels of his jacket. "Carter! Son! If you've ever done anything for me, do this now. I must go to the courthouse right this minute to see Jebediah."

Carter tried his best to calm and placate her. He was extremely worried by her seemingly hysterical condition.

"Mother, you know that's not possible. You truly are not well enough."

The strength in her bony little hands was incredible, considering her small size and weakened state. She held him to her with a tenacity he could hardly believe. The attendant was taking her blood pressure and the needle was soaring. He gave Carter an alarmed look.

"Carter!" she pleaded. "If you ever believed me before, believe me now. I must go to the courthouse! I am in my right mind. I know what I'm saying. Please, I beg you! It's a matter of utmost importance. Son, I implore you!"

He stared into her eyes. Her look was so intense and pleading. He realized she was perfectly lucid, even if very upset. His mind was in a quandary, thinking what was best to do for her. Her gaze never wavered. Finally, he relented.

Nodding to the driver, he said in a resigned voice, "Drive to the courthouse, please."

The driver nodded his head in acknowledgement and made a U turn. "Quickly!" Mrs. Manning rasped out. Almost exhausted, but relieved, she fell back against the pillow.

The baffled driver speeded up and turned on the sirens.

Chapter Thirty-Eight

The courtroom was typical of a small town county seat; not too small considering the present population, but built early in the century when hopes for greater growth were high. Oak benches and paneling, darkened through the years, prevailed everywhere. A large, round replica of the State Seal of Kansas hung with dignity high above the judge's banc.

The seating was occupied to capacity with anxious citizens, all faces showing various degrees of emotion and concern. Conversely, the center aisle divided the room into Black and Caucasian as if an invisible line had been drawn against the meshing of human existence.

The Honorable Richard Coleman was presiding. Directly beside him to his left, a rigid and extremely frightened Jebediah Jenkins sat in the witness box.

County Attorney, Thomas Hall, stood to begin his questioning. He was the great, great, great grandson of the builder of Freedom Hall; but his modern thinking was in no way similar to the liberal and compassionate tenets of his ancestor. In fact, most of the townspeople knew he was a veritable bigot, if not a downright racist. The case seemed tailor made to please him with its probable result, which would prove his own self-righteous credo. He wore the smug look of a man whose investigative work was already complete; and who was proceeding with the nonchalance and arrogance of someone confident, in this instance, of a "sure thing".

"Your Honor, Ladies and Gentlemen, the amount of condemning evidence we are about to put before you will prove to you that this young man you see seated there has committed crimes so horrible, so heinous, so cruel and greedy, that he should be indicted and put behind bars for a very long time...and, should the woman against whom these crimes were committed, the elderly, very much respected woman whom he beat unmercifully, who even this very minute only barely clings to life...should she DIE..."

Hall let the word and the thought gravitate and seep into the minds of those assembled. "Should she die, he should surely, in the name of all that's just, receive the death penalty!"

Many gasped as the impact of his words sank in. Some people sobbed at the harsh reality that seemed more than possible.

Attorney Hall paused for effect and stared gravely at his audience.

Jebediah closed his eyes and tried to take a deep breath. Fear gripped his heart with a mighty clenched fist. He realized the things he was about to say might condemn him as surely as if he refused to speak at all. But his Momma told him to always tell the truth, no matter what.

That's why he had asked to take the stand to tell his story. The real truth was always there, he felt. You couldn't hide it or deny it. It was forever the same. His lawyer, Mister Barker, had advised against Jeb testifying on his own behalf, but Jeb had insisted.

As scared as he was, Jeb looked out over the sea of faces before him and saw night and day expressions of anger and hatred, compassion and pity gazing at him from each side of the courtroom.

A small balcony above the rear seats was jammed to overflowing with his friends from school. Many of his classmates were seated there, even some of his teachers. He was stunned by their support. He figured they knew him probably better than anyone besides his family. They were the only integrated section, sitting shoulder to shoulder as a group, Cordelia among them. They reflected looks of incredible sympathy.

Jeb stared in amazed disbelief, for also among those integrated faces, sat Felix and Beulah Dalgren. And beside them, as incredible as it seemed, sat a grave and erect George Raven's Wing.

On the main floor, almost directly in front of him was his Momma, weeping quietly, his father's arm around her. Jeb steeled himself for what was coming. *Lord, stand by me now*, he prayed.

County Attorney Hall was pacing before him with a serious, frowning look of theatrical concentration. He cleared his throat dramatically, preparing to continue. But before he could begin, sirens sounded, coming louder and nearer to the courthouse. The screaming noise was so intense as to cause everyone to look around, commenting and wondering. Hall, prevented from speaking momentarily, was forced to wait for quiet to return. He seemed obviously impatient and completely miffed to have been summarily interrupted. The sirens stopped suddenly very close at hand. Relieved, Hall recouped his former demeanor and prepared to continue once more. When another disturbing commotion began within hearing just outside the double doors at the back of the courtroom, Hall looked outraged.

To everyone's astonishment, those doors flew open and two paramedics wheeled a stretcher down the center aisle. They were followed closely by a perplexed Carter Manning.

When the crowd realized what was happening, pandemonium broke out, and everyone began talking at once. Judge Coleman wielded his gavel like a large hammer, shouting "ORDER! ORDER IN THIS COURTROOM!" This was repeated several times. Gradually people quieted and the stretcher came to a stop in the middle of the courtroom, in front of the judge.

Mrs. Manning struggled to sit. Carter moved to support her in a more upright position. She peered at the Judge intently.

"Richard Andrew, is it you?" she asked, her voice surprisingly clear.

"Yes, Ma'am, Mrs. Manning. It's me." Remembering suddenly he was once a student in her English grammar class, he quickly corrected himself. "It is I, Mrs. Manning."

She motioned him to her; and the Right Honorable Richard Andrew Coleman stepped down from the bench and walked to her side. Mrs. Manning's thin little fingers clutched the front of his robe and pulled him down close.

"Richard Andrew, you remember that I have always been a woman of my word? A person of truth?" The Judge nodded his assent. "Well, I am about to tell you the truth, now, so help me God." Her voice was fading a little with her immense efforts. At this point, the entire assemblage was on its feet, straining to hear her.

Jeb was standing, too, in the witness box. He could hardly believe the pathetic, small figure on the gurney was really his Miz Manning. Her face was mottled and bruised, she had lost weight, and her hands were little bird-like claws. His heart ached. He thought for a moment he might become ill.

"Jebediah?" she asked. "Where is Jebediah?"

Jeb stepped down to walk to her. The bailiff moved immediately to restrain him; but the Judge shook his head and motioned him away. Jeb went to her side and she reached to take his hand. He held the tiny doll-like hand in both is large ones and patted it gently. He tried his best to smile confidently at her.

That very moment, looking into Jeb's kind, loving eyes, Carter realized with a jolt how completely wrong they had all been to doubt Jebediah Jenkins.

"Oh, Jebediah! I'm so sorry. I didn't know, I didn't know!" she wailed.

"Richard Andrew," her voice came a little stronger. "This is my friend, Jebediah Jenkins. He would never do anything to harm me. The person who broke into my home and nearly killed me was Hack Slater. It was HACK!"

With that statement, the entire courtroom became bedlam. Mrs. Manning had lain back depleted on the pillow of the stretcher; but she wouldn't let go of Jeb's hand. Carter motioned for the attendants to take his mother out. Judge Coleman stepped back to clear the way for them, waving the opposing attorneys to his chambers. Amos Barker, astounded though he was, had a grin as wide as a house. Defeated, Hall's grim countenance told another story.

People who had been cheering, shouting, and crying became mute and solemn, watching the strange procession exiting the court-room.

Carter walked on one side of Mrs. Manning and Jeb on the other. Jeb's mother came forward to kiss his cheek and hug him; but stepped back to let him go with her.

Outside, the people assembled quietly, respectfully and undivid-ed, now, on the courthouse lawn to watch this unique vignette played out to the end.

At the curb, Mrs. Manning squeezed Jeb's hand once more and murmured softly, "Good-bye, Jebediah. I have to go, now. My chariot awaits. Good luck, friend, and Godspeed."

It was at that moment, as he watched the ambulance drive away that Jeb knew he loved her. He didn't know it was the last time he would ever see her.

Chapter Thirty-Nine

It took several weeks for everyone and everything to settle down to a semblance of normal. Jeb had missed too much of school to graduate with his class, which was a total humiliation to him.

The school administration had been very understanding, taking into consideration the unusual circumstances. Tutoring was arranged so he could make up the work. Cordelia came over to his house almost every evening to help him study. Jeb was granted his diploma in mid-summer. His folks were still very proud of him; but he figured it just wasn't the same. He felt like he'd been robbed and beaten, too.

Carter came to his house and apologized for the unfortunate misunderstanding and the frightening ordeal he had endured. He offered Jeb his old jobs back, at the newspaper and even keeping everything up to snuff in Mrs. Manning's garden for the time when she would be able to come home.

"Thank you very kindly, Mister Carter. But I wouldn't feel quite right about doing that. What with Miz Manning not being there and everything." The boy looked whipped. "I talked to Mister Felix and Miss Beulah, and they already offered me a job helping them out at the nursery this summer," Jeb said sadly, head bowed, looking at his feet.

"I understand, Jeb. You've been through a really tough time, and none of it was your fault. I am sincerely so deeply sorry." Carter paused, lacking better words to express what he really felt for the young man. "Mother knows I intended to talk to you...she sends her regards...if that's any consolation." Carter shook his head, aching for Jeb.

Jeb's head came up and he looked directly into Carter's eyes. "Mister Carter, your Momma did a very brave thing on my behalf coming to that courtroom in her terrible condition. I'm never gonna forget that. Not ever!"

The pain Carter saw reflected in Jeb's eyes shocked him to the core. It was like looking at his mother. But this child had taken another kind of beating. Carter felt helpless and disconsolate. Jeb was gun-shy around him and Carter couldn't blame him for that. He had known this would probably be a futile effort; but he felt he owed it to Jeb to try.

Privately, Carter had offered to pay the Jenkins' legal costs. They had thanked him kindly and politely refused.

# Chapter Forty

Jeb tried to go and see Mrs. Manning several times. Once he brought a small bunch of Pansies in a little vase his mother gave him. The receptionist at the front desk told him she'd had a very restless night and was sleeping. They were asking visitors to come another day. He left the flowers, hoping they would be given to her.

Another time he went with a bright red, potted Geranium; but they said she had been taken to the clinic for x-rays and wouldn't return for an hour or more.

The last time he tried to pay her a visit, he'd taken her a "MISS-ING YOU" card, on which he'd written a short note. That time they told him she was having a water therapy session to help strengthen her muscles. After that, he was so discouraged he didn't go back anymore.

In late July, Jeb read in the newspaper where Hack was arrested in Lincoln, Nebraska. He had sold Mrs. Manning's car and was trying to get rid of her jewelry. Several jewelers and pawn shop owners became suspicious and notified the police.

Jeb already knew most of this because Amos Barker had called to inform him. After prolonged questioning, Barker said, the whole story had come out and Hack had confessed his guilt. Hack's girl-friend finally admitted she had lied to cover for him.

Hack's friend who owned the car was his accomplice. He had waited in the car while Hack perpetrated both the serious crimes of theft, and assault and battery. He had been the one to help Hack take the sun dial and the lid off the cistern. They planned to come back when all the uproar had simmered down and get the silver out of the cistern. They thought the sacks were so big, they would be too obvious and incriminating to carry with them, in case somebody noticed them. Their feeling was to get them out of the way temporarily and retrieve them later. Neither one had realized how deep the old cistern actually was.

The police had questioned Hack repeatedly. He eventually admitted working on the plan to rob Mrs. Manning for almost as long as he had worked for her. The opportunity to frame Jeb had come about strictly by accident.

His confessions became cocky and braggadocious. After the robbery, he had been smart enough to stay away from the main streets, being careful not to be spotted in the stolen car. On a side street, quite by chance, he had driven past Jeb's house and seen the Jenkin's car in front. It was then the really great idea came to him to leave a couple of pieces of the jewelry under the car's front seat. Better, he thought, to have the job definitely pinned on that punk, Jeb, and he could get away free and clear.

He hid Mrs. Manning's car in an old, unused garage for a few days in order to keep his routine looking normal until things cooled down. After all, he grunched ruefully, he had hoped the old lady was a goner.

Amos Barker had related all this information to Jeb and told him that most of the jewelry had been recovered. Jeb really was glad about that. Barker told him that all three had been arrested and indicted. Hack's trial was set for the middle of September. Jeb was double, triple, glad about that.

Chapter Forty-One

Early one evening late in August, Carter Manning telephoned Jeb at home. He informed him sadly that his mother had passed away the night before. He explained that her usually mobile lifestyle had been very restricted since the break in at the house. And because of all her injuries from the beating, she had been so inactive by comparison, and had contracted pneumonia. All the powerful, new wonder drugs had been to no avail. In her advanced age and weakened condition, she had been unable to fight it off. Carter said she had died quietly in her sleep around four o'clock in the morning. He told Jeb he would let him know when the funeral would be.

Jeb was completely stunned. He thanked Mister Carter for letting him know and hung up the phone, standing there in a daze for long moments.

He related this terrible news to his family stoically and left the house in a stupor. They also had been shocked and realized the depths of his personal sadness.

Jeb found the need to be by himself was overwhelming. He merely walked and walked for hours. He walked fast with the strength and stamina given only to the young, and with an intensity born mainly through shock and emotional trauma. He strode without consciously thinking, without purpose or direction, aimlessly, he felt, until he found himself in the country on Freedom Hall road, staring up at the limestone house where Mrs. Manning had lived as a child.

Jeb felt he knew this place well now, having been here with her, having heard it's fascinating history, having seen her home through the eyes of her childhood. Somehow, here, he felt much closer to her.

It was in that place, alone, by the side of the road that he let his sorrow expose itself. There, for a time, the tears of his grief overcame him. "Oh, Lord," he whispered softly, looking into the darkening summer sky, "Please take good care of my Miz Manning."

Chapter Forty-Two

Mrs. Manning's funeral had been attended by more people than any other funeral in Valleyville for years. She had made so many friends in her long life and done a great deal of good for a great many persons. Friends and relatives and even newspaper associates of years gone by came to pay their respects to the memory of a fine lady.

Jeb didn't go to the funeral. He read all about it in the paper. He was still very unsure of himself, still intimidated by what had happened to him, wondering how folks would react having him around. Besides, he didn't think he could keep his emotions in check. He just couldn't risk acting like a baby in front of all those people.

Two weeks later, Carter Manning called him to say that Mrs. Manning's will would be read at the house the following Monday, and requested that Jeb be present. Jeb thanked him nicely for including him, but said he'd sure feel real awkward being there, and he politely refused.

The day after that phone call, James Lanchaster, Mrs. Manning's lawyer, came to the house to see Jeb.

"Mrs. Manning spoke to me about you in June, Jeb. I think somehow she realized even then that she might not fully recover. She asked me specifically to come here and request to you personally that you be present when her will was read. You would, in reality, be honoring her wishes and the friendship the two of you had by attending the reading."

Jeb didn't know what to say; but he thought if Mrs. Manning had honestly wanted him to be there, he'd drum up his courage and go. He was trying mightily to act more grown up in spite of everything that had befallen him.

Because of the importance of the occasion, Jeb's folks let him take the family car. He drove up the long driveway to Mrs. Manning's house thinking he had nearly always walked it, except those few harrowing times when she had been driving. He smiled, wishing in spite of himself that she was doing the driving now.

Jeb glanced at the stand of Cedars across the far side of the property. Like glaring scars, what was left of this year's unsightly orange globs hung tenaciously from the branches. Those hateful two-host menaces reminded him of Hack. Hack was an ugly, evil person, a blight on the face of good people, spreading his terror and wrongs among everybody he touched.

Jeb still felt guilty that he had been the one to bring Hack here. He wished he could forgive him for what he had done, but his heart just wasn't that big or, in this case, forgiving. But that was now in the past and he'd best try and put it at the back of his mind.

As he drove on, he noticed that the lawn was mowed, but the edging had been carelessly done. There were some prominent weeds in the flower beds. *Wonder who's doing that sloppy work*, he thought ruefully, then quickly put that thought aside.

"That's not your nevermind any longer, Jeb," he muttered, admonishing himself.

Jeb parked by the big old Elm near the back porch where the two of them had sat companionably and talked so many times. He gazed at the peeling paint on the bench beside the back door and shook his head sadly. His fond memories were almost too poignant to recall.

Slowly he began to walk around to the front of the house past the cement lions guarding the entrance. He knew, for sure, he'd rather take a whippin' than be doing this.

It was Miss Evelyn who met him at the door. She smiled sweetly, sadly, and told him how glad she was to see him, how much she had missed him. He felt extremely awkward and out of his element.

The room was full of people, talking and chatting with each other. Family members, he supposed, and a few of Mrs. Manning's bridge "girls" he had seen come by the house every now and again, and some of the people from her church he reckoned.

He recognized a few faces. Gaddy Taylor was dressed to the nines and acting like the "queen bee", serving coffee to everyone. *You'd think it was a party rather than a wake*, he thought bitterly.

Miss Evelyn seemed to understand his feelings and drew him aside. "Jeb, I know you must be very sad about losing your friend,

Mrs. Manning. I truly empathize with you because I feel that way also. But we are so glad you agreed to come."

It was then that Carter extricated himself from a group of people and came to greet him. He put his arm around Evelyn's shoulders and said sincerely, "Jeb, you don't know how much it means to us for you to be here today. Thank you for coming." Jeb nodded, accepting what he realized was a sincere greeting.

"Evelyn and I wanted you to be among the first to know that we are going to be married in the spring," Carter said smiling. "I think Mother would have been pleased, too."

Jeb was surprised, but not overly surprised. *Looked like Miz Manning's little matchmaking plot worked out just fine. Wouldn't you know she'd have to be dead and gone before it took hold. Maybe she knows anyways,* he thought hopefully.

"That's real nice, Miss Evelyn, Mister Carter. Congratulations."

They both thanked him, looking into each other's eyes, smiling.

"Jeb," Evelyn said more seriously, "Carter and I have a favor to ask of you." This was a mystery to Jeb. He couldn't think what in the world he could do for them.

"Did you know that Daisy had also been hurt when the robbery happened?" Evelyn asked. "No, Ma'am," Jeb replied, shocked. He had been so preoccupied and frantic with everything that had happened, he'd forgotten all about Daisy.

"Yes, she was in pretty bad shape for a while; but fortunately she has recovered and is her old loving and inquisitive self again." Jeb felt a rush of relief at that news and couldn't begin to think how bad he would have felt if they'd lost good ol' Daisy, too.

It was at that instant that she found him. Jeb heard her soft roar before he felt the warm, fuzzy body brushing at his legs. He blinked back a sudden unexpected rush of tears, and picked up his old friend.

"Daisy has been with Evelyn and the children since she has recovered, Jeb. But unfortunately they can't keep her any longer. Evelyn's daughter, Jennifer, is extremely allergic to cats and it's causing quite a problem for her." Carter paused to let his words sink in. "Both of us would like you to have her, that is, if you want to take her...because we know she loves you so."

Jeb couldn't hide his pleasure at that request and hugged Daisy snugly against his chest. She was ecstatic to see him again and let him know in decibels.

"I'll be glad to take Daisy," Jeb said and thanked them. "My sister, Naomi, will be tickled to pieces. We'll be sure to give her a good home."

Jeb chose an upright chair in the far corner, out of the way by the door leading to the porch, Daisy in his lap squeezing her eyes shut in contentment.

He looked up and was startled to see George Raven's Wing standing near the front door just across the room. The old man leaned back against the wall with his arms folded across his chest, his eyes closed. It seemed as if he were chanting inside with the sound turned inward.

Jeb mentally sympathized. *He must feel as out of place and uncomfortable being here as much as I do.* Then George opened his eyes and stared straight ahead. Slowly, he looked around the room, his eyes coming to rest intently on Jeb. Jeb felt himself shrink. He could not look away from the old Indian, but was compelled to return his gaze. He stared in disbelief as the corners of George's mouth curled into a small, sad smile and he nodded to Jeb in recognition. Jeb was stunned, but very pleased. He returned George's nod and smiled hesitantly.

James Lanchaster cleared his throat and asked that everyone be seated. When all was quiet, he began to read. There were bequests to several people she had liked who had worked for her. Gaddy Taylor was one of them and preened proudly, happy when her name was announced.

Some personal things Mrs. Manning wanted given to close friends. Several bequests were to her church and some charities she favored. Jeb tried to let his mind wander to anywhere but where he was. He desperately wanted to go home.

Then Mr. Lanchaster read a bequest to George Raven's Wing. Because of Mrs. Manning's admiration for him and the friendship she and her husband had shared for so many years, she left a sum of money to him personally, to be used as he saw fit. For his people, for good works of any kind, or for himself. Her will stated that she trusted his judgement.

Carter Manning interrupted at this point to say that the silver which had been stolen had been damaged beyond repair. He, himself, had ordered it melted and refined. This bullion he had directed to be given to George's Crow Tribe to be used in some way as a tribute to George's years of faithful dedication to the memory of his Grandfather, Black Feather. George inclined his head slightly, acknowledging the honor in regal silence.

Jeb was impressed by the bequests to Mister Raven's Wing because he'd heard about the night at the cistern. All that had been one whale of a happening. But he felt so out of place here this day. He was getting nervous and impatient and just wanted to take Daisy and get the heck out.

"This is a personal letter dictated to me by Mrs. Manning in June, while she was in the Valleyville Nursing Facility. She requested that it be read to all those present here today." Mr. Lanchaster cleared his throat once more and read.

"To my friend, Jebediah Jenkins," Mr. Lanchaster quoted. Jeb was alert, now, head up but listening warily, eyes staring straight ahead.

"These past few years of our association and friendship have been a great pleasure for me. It gave me joy to get to know you and become your teacher in an area which I realize you have come to love, that of growing things.

"Therefore, I have instructed my attorney, James Lanchaster, to commence a trust fund in your name to afford you a college education, which I hope will be in the field of horticulture.

"I have also instructed him to deed to that trust a forty acre tract of land owned by me on the southwest outskirts of Valleyville, hoping that when your education is completed, you may wish to begin a business of your own as a nurseryman.

"These arrangements are to be with your agreement and approval.

"I return to you, one piece of personal property; the valued gift you gave to me at Christmastime. Please, keep it in memory of our friendship. I hope it will bring you pleasure and as many smiles as it did to me.

With sincere affection,
Amanda Lillian Manning"

Jeb stood up abruptly, dropping Daisy to the floor. He stumbled woodenly out onto the porch. He leaned his head against the house and tears streamed down his face. His body shook with wracking sobs. His grief was terrible and his wonder at her huge kindness awed him. Presently, he felt an arm across his shoulders, and Carter was beside him.

"It's all right, son. We all miss her, grieve for her. She was a very remarkable human being. My mother genuinely loved and respected you as her friend, Jeb; and this was her way of telling you so. She had so many good friends and all of them loved her in return." Carter was very moved himself and took a deep breath.

He squeezed Jeb's shoulders and said, "Our Mrs. Manning grew so much more than flowers in the garden of her heart."

Epilogue

His mother was at the cash register totaling up the days receipts and entering them into the neat ledger she kept faithfully every day.

It was spring. Business was picking up for the season. Customers were anxious to get their gardens planted and eager for his advice on how to get the best results.

His sister was spray-misting indoor plants which were artfully arranged under the large skylight. His wife, Cordelia, was stacking small boxes of weed and insect control on shelves near the bins of bulbs.

An ancient yellow cat lay sunning on the board planks of the front porch, keeping a lazy, watery eye on the man working outside next to the building. He wore jeans, a work shirt, and a black baseball cap with the name JEBEDIAH in gold letters above the bill. He looked up from where he was stacking sacks of peat, mulch, and fertilizer just outside the building, to see a woman emerge with an armload of bedding plants.

"Here now, Mrs. Coleman, let me carry those out to the car for you," he beamed his broadest smile.

"Why, thank you, Jebediah. I'd really appreciate that," she replied. She was one of his frequent and valued customers. It pleased him mightily that the Judge and his wife had never held a grudge against him since Mrs. Manning had exonerated him that day in court. The Judge's wife was an avid gardener. She always asked him what to do about this flower and that bush, calling him when there was some kind of bug or possible disease bothering her shrubs and vegetables. In that respect, she reminded him a lot of Mrs. Manning. He even felt he knew her well enough to tease her a bit about her careful over-mothering of all her prized flowers. He deposited the plants carefully in the back of her car and waved as she drove away.

Then slowly he turned and gazed at the source of his deep pride and joy. The single story building was of moderate size, with barn red siding and a shake shingled roof, and several glass greenhouses attached at the rear of the structure. Outside to the left was a lattice-work arbor with sawhorses beneath, bearing boards across the top to support the many flats of bedding plants in every color imaginable. A rainbow's slash of wonder met his eye. To the right was a barn-like structure which housed tools and served as a storage shed. And, yes, quite a ways out back of that barn was a large, smelly compost heap. He smiled and shook his head thinking he didn't know how he would manage without that odoriferous, "magic" pile.

Flanking either side of the entrance walk, a white cement elephant stared back at him, with cement baskets on their backs, filled to capacity in red and white Geraniums. His "sentimental sentries", Mrs. Manning would have called them and laughed at their private joke. Jeb chuckled softly at his fancy in remembering his dear mentor.

"We did it, Miz Manning," he said softly. "We really, truly, actually did it, Old Friend! Lord, be praised!"

A sheen of tears veiled his eyes as he sought the sign over the front door which always made him feel about to burst with pride whenever he looked at it:

> *Certified Horticulturist and Nurseryman*
> JEBEDIAH JENKINS' GROWING THINGS

The End